# My Army

# Ranger

## The Texas Kincaids Book 4

# Bonnie Phelps

Lilac Lace Press

ebook ISBN: 978-0-9989303-4-3

Paperback ISBN: 978-1-7329613-0-2

Cover Designed by GetCovers

Bonnie's website: www.bonniephelpsauthor.com

Contact Bonnie at: bonnie@bonniephelpsauthor.com

## DEDICATION

To my amazing husband for all of his support and for introducing me to the meaning of true romance! To my daughters for all their encouragement and support. To all the amazing men and women who serve or have served in our military.

# Contents

# Chapter One

♥

THE HAIRS ON THE back of Crystal Kincaid's neck tingled. Goosebumps puckered her arms. She stopped dead in her tracks, right there on the main street of one of the small, Texas Hill Country towns west of Austin and San Antonio. A few steps later, her companions paused and looked back. Curiosity and concern furrowed their brows.

So much for a relaxing shopping trip with her cousins' wives.

"Crystal, what's wrong?" Lauren asked, reaching out her hand.

"Sweetheart, you look like you've seen a ghost." Ashley closed the gap between them and slipped an arm around Crystal's waist.

"Is it him?" Fiona asked as she scanned the street.

The pressure binding Crystal's chest lessened. How had she gotten so lucky? Her friends—family by marriage—were ready to do battle for her. She'd grown up with their husbands Nate, Zach, and Josh. Her dad and their dad were brothers, and the two ranches shared a property line.

"It's nothing. I just had a funny feeling. Nerves?" Crystal lifted one shoulder and hoped her smile looked rueful. "Ever since Jonathan started his campaign to win me back, I've been jumpy. Maybe I shouldn't have put so much jalapeno salsa on my enchilada?"

"You make light of it, but Jonathan's behavior worries me. And that *campaign*... is called stalking," Lauren, Nate's wife, said. "Even though you only dated him a few times, he's not taking no for an answer. I still think you should contact the police."

"It's stopped since I changed my phone number and moved to Austin." Crystal shifted the shopping bag she carried to her other hand. "If it starts up again, I promise I'll alert the police. Most likely, he's lost interest."

"Hmmm..." Lauren didn't sound convinced.

"You're welcome to stay with Josh and me whenever you want," Fiona said. "We've got plenty of room and would feel better knowing you're not alone."

Crystal squeezed Fiona's hand. "I appreciate the offer, but I'm fine." She smiled at each of her friends. "Really." Casually brushing her golden-brown hair from her face, she glanced up and down the street. The feeling she was being watched hadn't gone away, and her stomach tightened.

Unable to suppress a gasp, Crystal swallowed hard as she spotted the man across the street. Like marionettes, her friends' heads swiveled to follow her gaze. Together they eyed the tall, dark-haired man with the military cut. No sharp angles or chiseled features formed his face but there was nothing soft about him. He possessed a body that had obviously seen tough conditioning, and an attitude that screamed 'don't mess with me'. He was leaning against the wall across the street.

Ashley, Zach's wife, placed a hand on her very pregnant belly and whispered, "*Who is that*?"

"Cam." Crystal's voice sounded like she was in church. Hushed. Reverent. She couldn't see his deep brown eyes from this distance but sensed them boring into her with the intensity of the business end of a gun. She'd heard her childhood friend—and the boy she'd had a crush on for as long as she'd been interested in boys—was back in the area but seeing him caught her by surprise.

"Wait a minute," Fiona leaned close and their cheeks brushed. "That's Cam? Josh's best friend Cam? Josh and Dave had drinks with him the other night."

Crystal's knees felt like mush and butterflies batted against her heart. "Yes. One third of the triple threat." A chuckle escaped past the hand covering her mouth. "Josh, Dave, and Cam. They were inseparable." Raising her arm, she motioned him to join them.

Pushing off from the wall, he crossed the street, his gait not as smooth as it used to be.

Her throat constricted. She knew he'd lost a leg in Afghanistan and hadn't been out of Walter Reed that long. Hearing about his injury was one thing. Seeing him made it real.

Stopping in front of her, she thought at first he might hug her but he shoved one hand in the pockets of his well-fitting jeans instead. "Hey Caramel, how're ya doing?" In what she read as an involuntary movement, his knuckles gently grazed her cheek, and his smile actually reached his eyes. That lasted about two seconds before his expression shuttered and his hand fell to his side. Still treating her like a kid sister.

Fiona mouthed, *Caramel*?

The raised brows of her three friends told her she might as well explain. "From the time I was little, I followed Josh and his friends around like an awkward puppy. Cam kept a supply of caramels, my favorite candy, in his pocket, doling them out when I needed cheering. He started calling me Caramel, and the nickname stuck." She shook her head and smiled as pleasant memories flowed past, slow and easy like a summer creek. Cam had always been her knight in shining armor. "I don't know how you guys put up with me all those years."

A grin tugged at the corner of his mouth and he ducked his head. "You and your million questions *were* a burden." He grunted when she punched his arm. "But you kept us out of trouble..." He grinned. "Mostly." His face sobered. "You haven't answered my question. How're you doing?"

Ashley put a hand on Crystal's arm. "It looks like you two have some catching up to do, and I need to get home." She stuck out her hand. "I'm Ashley, Zach's wife. I hate to run, but it was nice to meet you."

Lauren and Fiona each introduced themselves and which Kincaid brother was their husband.

Cam shook each of their hands. "Nice meeting each of you. Those Kincaid men are lucky bas—" Cam cleared his throat. "Devils. Fiona, I'll see you this weekend. Josh invited me over for a barbeque."

"He did, did he?" Fiona put a hand on her hip and pointed a finger at Cam. "Someone who has his buddy's back would text his friend and suggest he pick up flowers for his wife." With a final wave, the trio turned and strolled off.

Chuckling Cam said, "Josh has his hands full with that one."

The warmth of the affection she felt for each of her cousins and their wives, created a warm bubble in her chest. "None of my cousins are going to get anything past their wives."

Nodding, Cam stepped closer and hooked one finger with hers lifting her hand. "Let's go get some coffee and talk."

His touch sent a jolt of electricity up her arm, and heat tinged her cheeks. "I know you've talked to Josh so assume you've heard about the unwanted attention I'm getting."

"I'd say *unwanted* is an understatement." He took the shopping bag she carried. "You moved from San Antonio to Austin. You changed your phone number, got a new email address, and deleted all your social media."

She felt his scrutiny and offered a feeble smile. "I was going to move anyway because I got a teaching job with the Austin School district that I'd applied for last year." Sucking in a cleansing breath, Crystal continued, "I'd be lying if I said this situation didn't spook me. The uncertainty of never knowing when he'd show up, the creepiness of constantly being tracked..." She shuddered, and Cam slung an arm across her shoulders just as he stumbled.

Every muscle in his body coiled tighter than the spring on her garden gate—the one that slapped her in the butt if she didn't move quickly enough. Helplessly, she watched his face contort into humiliation and anger before he schooled it into determination.

"Sorry, I'm still getting used to this thing." He slapped his left leg. "My physical therapist says it will be a while before I can run a full marathon, but she swears I can do it."

"You've always done anything you set your mind to." She paused, "You rarely let anything stop you." This must be killing him. He'd always been so athletic. Horseback riding. Helping her cousins herd cattle on her uncle's ranch, as well as her own. Even a little bronc riding thrown in because that's what Texas boys did.

His jaw clenched then he worked it like someone had punched him. "I'm not going to let this," –again he slapped his leg— "slow me down. I'm jogging up to three miles a day now." He held the door and ushered her inside the small, old-fashioned coffee shop. "Also got a motorcycle, so I can ride with Josh and Dave."

Her head whipped around. "Isn't that dangerous? The three of you horsing around?" She clamped her mouth shut because she'd almost added, *given your situation*.

Cam shrugged and he held out a chair for her. "You still take your coffee with lots of cream… or are you into those fancy latte things?"

"Regular coffee is fine and yes, I still like lots of cream." She started to rise. "Can I help?"

He put a hand on her shoulder and eased her back. "I can do it." His voice held an edge, sharp and pointy as a spear.

"I know you can." She patted the table. "I'll wait right here." Sighing she watched him walk toward the counter. Unlike her father, Cam hadn't given up. He seemed determined to figure out a way forward.

·♥·♥·♥·♥·♥·

CAMERON RODRIGUEZ, YOU'RE AN *idiot*. He wanted to bang his head against the wall and let the pain consume him. He should have kept his distance like he'd planned. But there she'd been. Soft curls hanging to the middle of her back, tousled by the mild breeze. Her sweet oval face pinched with worry as she talked to her friends. She'd tried to be casual, but he'd seen her scanning the street, that lithe body of hers ready to take flight. What else could he do but go to her? Look after her, like he'd done all his life?

Who was he kidding? He'd lost his leg over a year ago. Now he was half a man. Was he still capable of protecting her? He'd have to do what he'd always done... love her from afar and remind himself that she deserved so much more than someone whose own father had left as soon as he was born. A disappointment from day one.

After placing their order, he stepped to the side to wait. Watching her, bent over her phone, he admired the understated beauty she'd become. No longer the gangly kid, all arms and coltish legs. More than anything though, it was her empathy and basic decency that drew him to her. After her dad's accident, she'd stepped up—probably more than she should have at her young age—and shouldered a big chunk of responsibility for running her family's ranch. He'd done what he could to ease her burden. Helping with roundups and small repairs when he could. She'd let so much of her childhood pass her by. He'd seen her stoic in the face of her father's bitterness but also saw the pain and guilt she'd tried to hide.

The mugs clinked as he removed them from the tray and set them on the table along with a piece of blueberry pie and two forks. "It looked too good to pass up," he said, feeling like a randy teenager trying to impress her.

"I probably shouldn't splurge on the calories, but you always could talk me into stuff. Remember when you guys went cliff diving at the old quarry?" she asked picking up a fork. "You held my hand and jumped with me. That was the only reason I had the courage."

Cam chuckled. "Yeah, I do. I'm sure they heard your scream in the next county." He wrapped his lips around a bite of pie. "Josh said he talked you into riding with him on his motorcycle. Gotta say that piece of news shocked the hell out of me. You've always played it so safe."

She turned a pensive gaze on him. "I knew Josh wouldn't take any chances with me on his bike." Her lips lifted in a grin. "Once I relaxed, it was exciting. I realized how much I've missed. Maybe it's time to live with a little more boldness."

"I'm glad to hear it. You deserve to have fun." He took a sip of his coffee. "So why were you shopping *here* today? Isn't this a little out of the way?" Watching her smile disappear into the shadows, he gripped his fork until his knuckles whitened.

"Jonathan owns an insurance agency in our hometown and lives nearby. I didn't want to chance running into him. Since we all came from different directions, this was a good middle ground." Her lips pinched together as she shrugged. "Besides, Ashley wanted to visit a furniture-maker here to talk about something for the baby's room." She chased a bite of pie around the plate.

Cam's pulse pounded in his ears and anger burned in his gut. "So, basically this guy has turned your life upside down." He put down his coffee and covered her hand with his. "What's he doing that scares you so much?"

She shrugged and a surge of protectiveness swept over Cam. "Crystal." He squeezed her hand and gentled his voice. "I'd like to help. Talk to me."

Inhaling deeply, she looked down at the table. "At first, it was just annoying. Constant phone calls—like twenty a day—begging me to take him back. When I stopped answering, he left messages. Those messages and emails became more desperate. When he showed up at the preschool where I worked, I got really nervous. I'd die if anything happened to one of the children."

Her voice came out on a sigh. "According to Lauren—she's a psychologist—Jonathan's behavior is typical of an obsessive stalker. Even though we only dated a few times, he fixated on me." She lifted her head and gazed into his eyes. He felt the familiar pull of longing, the one he needed to suppress. "I'd always assumed a stalker had a relationship with his victim, but apparently that's not always the case. Stalkers have been known to pick their victims at random because there's something about them that triggers the stalker's desire to possess."

Her free arm gripped her waist and Cam wanted to toss a chair through the window. His army training pushed those emotions to a place where he could deal with them later. Now, his mind focused like a diamond cutter on the issue at hand. "Even though you haven't heard from him in a while, you're afraid he might have found you?"

"I don't know. It's just a feeling in the last few days. Like I'm being watched." Crystal pinched the bridge of her nose.

Crystal moistened her lips and Cam's gut clenched as he tracked the movement of the tip of her tongue.

"Enough about me," she said. "How in the world did you end up here today?"

"My mom's set to retire soon, and I'm looking for a house for her. A couple of friends live here, and it's close enough to Austin that I can visit often. I'd just finished looking at a few properties and was mulling over which to show her when I saw you." He smiled and when she returned it, a weight lifted off his chest. She didn't have to know he'd heard she'd be here today and wanted to make sure she'd be safe.

"Your mom is lucky to have you," Crystal said.

"I'm glad I'm in a position to do something to make her life easier. She's worked hard all her life and sacrificed so much for me. It's hard being a single mom." He heard the gruffness in his voice but was pleased that Crystal thought well of him.

Crystal glanced at her watch as he put the last bite of pie in his mouth. "Wow, it's getting late. I need to get going." She slid her hand from under his. "Since we both live in Austin now, we should get together sometime." They exchanged phone numbers and emails.

Cam stood and held her chair for her. "I'll walk you to your car."

He tucked her hand into the crook of his arm. When they reached her car, Crystal gasped. His arms instinctively went around her, and she buried her face in his chest. Scrawled on the hood of her car in thick, black marker were the words, *You're Mine*.

# Chapter Two

♥

"I've been so careful. How did he track me down?"
The pressure felt like she'd dived one hundred feet below
the ocean's surface. If Cam hadn't been here, she'd have
taken off and kept running until her lungs couldn't draw
another breath and her legs couldn't move. She wiped her
tear-stained cheeks against his soft cotton t-shirt, feeling
the hard muscle beneath as she drew Cam's scent deep
into her lungs. If only staying in his embrace could make
Jonathan disappear.

"He probably followed one of your friends, figuring
they'd eventually lead him to you." She felt him raise his
head and look around. "Small town like this... hopefully
someone noticed something." Cam placed a finger under
her chin and lifted her face until the only thing she could
see was his dark eyes. "You do know we need to go to the
police?"

Crystal nodded, pulled her cell phone out of her purse,
and snapped a few photos. By the time they'd visited the
police department, the sun had set. While the police understood her concern and sympathized with her plight,

legally, it was only a case of vandalism. She couldn't prove Jonathan did it and not some kid.

"I'd hoped to be home before dusk," Crystal glanced at the darkening sky. "I try to avoid being out after dark by myself." She smiled and tried to put on a brave face, even though her stomach had turned in to a hard ball.

"You're not going to be by yourself. I'm following you home." Cam's tone brooked no argument.

"You really don't have to go to all that bother. I'm sure you have a million other things to do."

"It's no bother. It's what friends do. Chances are he's around hoping to follow you home." Cam lightly grasped her upper arms. "If I'm trailing you, it will be much harder for him to go undetected." He bent his head so his face was even with hers. "Let me do this."

She swallowed past the lump in her throat. "Thanks." She drew a deep breath and set her chin. "My insides are quaking, so I appreciate the company." She put a hand to her stomach.

Slowly his lips met hers. Gentle. Careful. Reassuring. The kiss was hardly more than a breath, but it was everything she'd ever dreamed a kiss from Cam would be. The power and integrity of the man touched her soul in that brief moment. "My truck's on the next block. Drop me off there and I'll follow you."

A car did try to follow them, but on the two-lane country road, it was easy to spot. Cam flashed his brights behind her and slowed. The car turned off at the next crossroad. No way to tell if it was Jonathan. The sedan wasn't the SUV he usually drove, but that didn't mean he wasn't behind the wheel.

Crystal was a bundle of nerves by the time she reached the driveway of her small rental house. She pulled into the garage and waited. Was it Cam's intent to simply escort her and ensure no one followed, or did he plan to come in and check for boogeymen? She hoped for the latter. She wasn't looking forward to going into a dark house by herself.

When he got out of his car and limped toward her, she sagged with relief. A quick stab of guilt dulled that relief. His leg was obviously hurting, yet in typical Cam fashion, he'd ignore it if it meant helping someone.

"I'm glad to see you've got a garage and park your car in it. Do you keep the door into the house locked?" he asked. He must have seen her scowl because he added, "People with garage door openers often figure that's enough protection." Arms crossed and stance wide, he surveyed the area.

"Yes, I keep the inner door locked. Josh insisted. He also added a deadbolt, as well as the regular lock." She captured her bottom lip between her teeth. "Do you want to come in and look around?"

His face softened, and he smiled. "Still worried about little green monsters under your bed?"

"No."

He raised one brow and she sighed.

"Okay. Maybe."

"I don't see any exterior security cameras or lights. Do you plan to get some?"

"I've been meaning too. The landlord said I could, as long as I don't make any structural or wiring changes." Cam must think she was a complete incompetent and maybe he was right. "Josh said he'd help me figure out what I need." She shrugged. "It's been over three weeks since I moved and last heard from Jonathan. I guess I hoped this would all go away." She pushed the button to lower the garage door—with it open, she felt too exposed.

"You're in luck. Security systems are my specialty." He paused, and she didn't like the set of his mouth. "You had to know he would find you. It's not like you moved three thousand miles away and cut off all ties to your family and friends." He reached for her hand and squeezed it. "You can't ignore this."

"I know." With her hand in his, she let his warmth and strength seep into her. "It's all so overwhelming."

His big hands framed her face, his fingers tangled in her hair, and his lips meeting hers promised tenderness and safety. Everything tingled where he touched—the most delightful, arousing sensation she'd ever felt, and his taste... intoxicating. His fingers worked magic on her scalp and a blinding light filled her vision. Even after her eyelids fluttered shut, it was there. She was drifting out to sea on a riptide, lost, yet buoyed by a life jacket that let her know she was secure.

This was exactly where she was meant to be.

Slipping her arms around him, her fingers ranged over his back, testing the contours and ridges of his corded muscles. Power and restraint greeted her touch. She was tired of him holding back. She wanted to be the kind of woman who inspired his wildness. By the time the tip of his tongue traced her lips, her knees had grown weak, and her heart beat to a hypnotic, sensuous rhythm. She'd waited so long for him to respond to her as a woman—not Josh's younger cousin.

When he raised his head, he stepped back, all business, but the color in his cheeks indicated he wasn't unaffected. "Let's go inside so I can get a count of windows and doors. Then I'll walk your perimeter to identify any bushes we might want to trim and how many cameras and motion-sensor lights you should have."

Entering the kitchen, she was pleased to see she hadn't left dirty dishes in the sink. "Can I get you some coffee or bottled water?"

"No thanks. I'm fine." He pulled out his phone and opened a program.

She tracked his gaze as he studied the room and entered notes into his phone. Following him from room to room was like following a stranger. The lonely boy she'd known growing up had morphed into a hard, disciplined, military man. He had a way about him that epitomized stillness. Silent and on high alert, he was on a mission. His eyes turned hawkish and calculating. She could almost see thoughts being shuttled into their proper slots like keys into old-fashioned pigeonholes. He examined locks, tested the slide of windows, asked which windows she never opened, and typed in lots of notes.

Once outside, he arced a high-powered flashlight he'd retrieved from his vehicle over the roofline of the house. At the same time, he examined her yards—front, side, and rear—and checked the latches on her gate. All the while his fingers tapped on his keypad.

Back inside and seated at the dining room table beside him, anxiety placed a stranglehold on her lungs. How bad was her security? How easily could someone invade the space she has just started to believe was safe? The knuckles on her entwined fingers turned white as she pressed her palms together.

Cam laid his hand over hers, comforting and soothing. "Have you ever thought about getting a couple of dogs?"

She pounded her chest with her fist as she coughed.

His chuckle wove through her and loosened anxiety's hold. "Not exactly what I expected you to say, but no, I hadn't thought about it. I'd feel guilty if I didn't give it the attention it deserved."

"That's why you get more than one, so they keep each other company. Also, a dog is the best security system on the market." He patted her hand and sat back. "I'll make a list of items I want to install and what modifications I'll need to make to the property, so you can pass it along to your landlord." He nudged her foot under the table. "Don't worry, other than upgrading a few locks, drilling a few holes, and trimming a few bushes, the structural impact is minimal."

"What's all this going to cost?" she asked. "I won't get my first paycheck until after school starts next month."

"Don't worry about it." His voice sounded like a growling bear.

"How much?" She could be stubborn too.

"I know a guy, so less than a thousand bucks. You can pay me back later." His eyes narrowed as though daring her to argue then he shrugged. "I got a decent separation from the Army so can afford to front you the money."

"But aren't you buying a house for your mom? I don't want to mess that up." She chewed on her cheek. "And do you have time? Aren't you looking for work?"

"The money's not a problem, and the job thing is already covered. Josh and Dave's company, JSM Cyber Security, hired me. I asked to wait a month before starting, so I've got the time."

When she opened her mouth to rebut his claim, his scowl deepened. "Okay," she said. "You can lend me the money." She scowled right back at him. "But I'm not a charity case. I just hadn't planned to leave my old job until just before school started. Then I had to rent this furniture and the house deposits, so finances are a little tight."

"Why are you renting furniture? Didn't you have stuff at your old place?" He scratched his head.

"I did, but it's all stored at my parents' ranch for now. My brother and cousins moved it out after I left, so Jonathan wouldn't know where I went." She swallowed hard. "I snuck out like a thief in the night." A sob bubbled in her throat. "I guess I'll have to stay away from everyone for a while since he is obviously looking for me."

Cam stood, pulling her with him, and wrapped her in his embrace. His hands rubbed her back comforting her. Relaxing against him, she'd be more than happy to let the world stay on its own side of the wall.

Her phone dinged that a text had arrived. She sighed, the spell broken, and plucked it off the table. Tapping the message icon, her knees buckled, and the phone slipped from her fingers. Cam caught her, almost losing his balance in the process, but he fought for control, and eased her into a chair.

He scooped her phone off the floor, and suddenly Crystal understood the saying, *murderous expression*. "I guess there's no doubt Jonathan was there today." Cam scrolled through the images of Crystal shopping with her friends, meeting up with him, the two of them at coffee, and finally standing in front of her car. "You didn't see him at all today?"

She shook her head and reached for the phone. Their fingers touched, and she felt the now-familiar electricity, surprised anything could get past the numbness. After staring at the message for a moment, she looked up at him with fresh tears in her eyes. "He accused me of cheating on him?" Folding into herself with her elbows on her knees, she tunneled her fingers through her hair. "Why is he doing this? I told him in no uncertain terms that I never

17

wanted to see him again." She tried to swallow but her mouth was dry. Her nice, safe, world had flown out the window.

Cam pulled her to her feet and gathered her in his arms rocking her back and forth. His voice whispered in her ear over and over. "It's going to be okay. I'm here for you."

When her body finally stopped shaking, he said, "I'm spending the night here. No telling if he's found out where you live." He lifted her chin. "I need to grab a few things and pick up my dogs. You're coming with me."

"How did he get my phone number? Only family and close friends have it. None of them would have given it out..." That's as far as her thoughts could go. Blank.

Cam brushed a hand over her hair. "There are ways. Most likely hacked the computer of one of your family members when they clicked on a link or document he sent them. He even could have made it look like it came from someone else." He took her hand and picked up her purse. "Here you go. Come on."

Feeling limp as a dishrag, Crystal accepted the purse he handed her and followed him out the door.

# Chapter Three

♥

Quiet descended in Cam's truck on the drive to his place. Not a companionable quiet but one shrouded in dread. The only thing she'd said was what she wanted to eat when they stopped at a Chinese restaurant for take-out.

Cam didn't know much about stalkers. Mostly what he knew were the ones who made the news. The ones who'd broken into a celebrity's home or murdered the woman being stalked—when it was too late to do anything. His hands gripped the steering wheel. He'd have to do some research and find out what he was up against. He accepted he wasn't the warrior he'd once been, but he'd fight with everything in him to protect Crystal. While physical therapy had helped him learn to use his artificial limb, he still had a long road ahead.

Reaching across the console, he'd only meant to massage her scalp with his fingertips like he'd done when they were kids. That had always relaxed her, but she jumped a foot and placed a hand on her chest, breathing hard. Her head whipped around, and her eyes were wild.

Cam cursed under his breath. "I'm sorry," he said. "I didn't mean to scare you.

She exhaled softly as she eased back into her seat. "No. I was slipping off to a place I really don't want to go." One corner of her mouth lifted in a shaky smile. "You brought me back."

He didn't know what to say. She looked at him, waiting expectantly. He needed to say something. "You're going to be okay. You're strong." He wanted to smack his head against the steering wheel.

"Regardless," she squeezed his arm. "You've always grounded me. When my first instinct is to hide, I need a push, every once in a while, to get out of my own way."

He pulled into his driveway, grimacing as he climbed out of his truck. Sometimes his hip cramped and made walking painful, and then there was the phantom pain, but he wasn't going to live on pain pills like some of the guys in his unit. He'd seen where that could lead.

She caught up to him as he limped to the front door. God, he wanted to stretch out on the sofa and give his body a chance to recuperate. He was sure she'd noticed his limp but didn't say anything, just held his hand and smiled encouragement. His head bowed in relief. He couldn't abide pity.

Opening the door, he flipped on the lights and smothered a grin when she spotted the gym equipment filling his living room. He supposed he could have put it in one of the bedrooms, but he liked looking out the front window while he worked out. It helped pass the time and made him feel connected to the world.

If he ever wanted to be even a smidgen of the man he'd once been, he needed to push himself. His physical therapist counseled patience. Given the extent of his injuries, he was ahead of schedule. He was jogging again, maybe like an old man, but jogging, increasing the distance a little every week. His stride was gradually smoothing out. Still, it felt like he'd been marking time forever.

"I see you've taken a chapter out of the happy home-maker decorating handbook." She batted her lashes and chuckled, dragging him back to the present.

"Yeah, I thought this," his elbow indicated the equipment, "gave the place a lived-in look." He took her hand and led her toward the great room at that back of the house. "I need to let the dogs in and feed them before we take off."

Her double take when she entered the great room was priceless. Biting back another grin he watched her look over her shoulder into the living room then sweep over the room they were in, a puzzled frown on her face.

"This is nice," she said. Her eyes narrowed, and a hand fisted on her hip. "Did your mom pick out this furniture?"

A deep belly laugh rumbled through the room. It felt good to laugh again. "Excuse me? Are you implying that I don't have any taste?" He laughed again at her sheepish expression. "When I bought my television, the store had this set up around it." He shrugged. "I liked it, so I took it all."

Her fingers trailed along the back of the tan, L-shaped leather sofa and the burgundy leather recliner as she followed him to the sliding door. The three dogs sat patiently waiting and didn't enter until he gave them a hand signal. She made a chuffing noise.

"What?" He heard the exasperation in his voice and wished he'd kept his mouth shut.

"I'm amazed. The dogs you had when we were kids were..." She seemed to be searching for the right word.

21

"A bunch of hooligans?" he finished.

"I was going to say rambunctious, but your description works."

His mind wandered back over the years. He'd been a hellion. Angry at the world. Angry at the father who didn't want him. His mom had put up with a lot. No telling where he'd be if he hadn't fallen in with Josh and Dave in elementary school. "The Army taught me the value of discipline."

"Let me introduce you to the guys." He snapped his fingers and pointed to his feet. The dogs trotted over and sat. He scratched the head of a Lab/Shepard mix and had to swallow past the lump in his throat. "This is Max. Got him when I started physical therapy at Walter Reed. We've been through a lot." He rubbed the silky ears of a little beagle. "This is Scooter. He flunked out of bomb sniffing school, and military guys get the first chance to adopt." He shrugged. "Max needed a friend." The third dog, a terrier mix, raised its chin so Cam could run his hand along his neck. "And this little guy is Bandit. The local dog rescue group had him outside a pet store and I couldn't resist."

Crystal crouched down and let each dog sniff her before petting them. "They're wonderful. I can see why you fell in love with them. Luckily for you, my lease allows pets, so there won't be a problem."

"I'm going to gather up my stuff. Why don't you feed them and then set out some plates for us, so we can eat?" He put out his hand to help her up. After a few brief instructions about where to find things, he picked up the television control and turned on the local news. "Feel free to change the channel."

"What is it with guys and big-ass television sets? Poor eyesight?" she asked.

"Look out lady. You're getting close to crossing a line." The easy banter they'd developed as children took him back to the time dreams were still possible. "I think it's the experience. When we're watching sports or a movie," he lifted one shoulder, "guys like to feel like we're right in the middle of the action. The sound should be able to rumble through us like a herd of elephants."

"Bet your neighbors love that."

Playfully he dug his knuckles into her scalp and smiled when she ducked. "Don't give me a hard time." He turned her toward the kitchen and swatted her butt. "I'll just be a few minutes." Whistling a tune, he headed down the hall to his bedroom.

Pulling his duffle bag off the shelf in the closet, he packed it with precisely folded underwear from the bureau, a couple pairs of jeans, short-sleeved shirts, and socks. In the bathroom he filled his kit with his personal hygiene products. As an afterthought, he tossed in a bar of soap. He wasn't about to use any girly products Crystal might have on hand.

Unplugging his laptop, he loaded it into his computer bag. He grabbed the firewall unit he used to deter hacking and tucked it beside his laptop. He didn't want anyone doing unto him what he planned to do unto others. Lastly, he stowed his firearm lockbox in his duffle, and he was ready to go.

Leaving the two bags by the front door, he followed his nose to the kitchen. She'd set out plates and glasses on the small pine table and opened the white Chinese food carry-out cartons. He paused and watched her sitting at the table frowning at her phone. Massaging his forearms where the muscles had bunched in tight knots, he visualized the creative ways he knew to hurt a man without leaving a mark. If push came to shove, he figured he'd regained enough agility to do some serious damage against someone like Jonathan. He sniffed and his stomach rumbled. Crystal must have heard him because she looked up.

She motioned him over. "Let's not let this food get cold."

The wooden chair scraped against the tile floor as he sat beside her, their shoulders touching. Taking the phone from her, he laid it face down on the table. "Give it a rest for a while."

"I just don't see how he could have gotten close enough to take these pictures without any of us noticing." She reached for the phone and Cam placed his hand over hers. His throat tightened when he felt the quiver beneath his palm.

"Desperate people can accomplish a lot that seems impossible to most of us. War taught me that." He pushed the phone out of her reach and picked up his chopsticks. "How's your family doing?" Cam accepted her assessing gaze without flinching. She finally picked up her own chopsticks.

"Did I mention in one of my letters that Wayne passed his veterinary licensing exam and joined Nate's practice?" She asked.

Cam nodded and scooped some Kung Pao Chicken into his mouth.

"It's nice to have my brother working with his cousin. Keeps him close to home." She toyed with her Beef and Asparagus. "Mom's her usual serene self. I swear, nothing breaks that woman's stride."

His body relaxed into the memory. "I can still see her on her horse quietly issuing orders to the ranch hands. Never had to raise her voice, but the guys sure did jump when she spoke." He also remembered the bitterness on her dad's face. "How's your dad? Last time I saw him he was still fighting that wheelchair."

He was glad to see she'd finally put some food in her mouth and waited patiently while she chewed. Her face cleared, and she actually smiled.

"Better. I think he's making peace with being paralyzed from the waist down. Getting back on a horse made a difference. He's not crazy about the hoist, but when he's in that saddle, he's a new man. It killed him to take a back seat in running the ranch."

She looked down quickly and fiddled with her chop-sticks. He watched a lone tear track down her cheek, and his heartrate slowed.

"Aw Caramel, it wasn't your fault. The accident could have happened any time. Ranching's dangerous."

"But he was out looking for me. If I hadn't run off in a snit..."

"What? He'd never have been hurt? You've got to stop thinking like that." Cam scrubbed a hand over his face when she cringed. "Sorry for snapping." He chucked her under the chin. "None of us can know what's going to happen, or how we're going to handle the shit that lands in our laps."

He swiveled and put a hand on each of her shoulders. "Bitterness. Shaking your fists at the gods. Believing life has treated you unfairly." He shrugged. "Sometimes that's part of the process but it sounds like he's coming out on the other side."

He could see she wanted to ask if that's how he felt about his injury. He turned back to his food, and with his forearms resting on the table, hunched over his plate. "Don't." He supposed it was natural for her to wonder.

But at this point he didn't have any answers. He hoped he wasn't like her dad but there were days. At this point, he was only a shell of his former self. Until he could be the man she deserved, he had nothing to offer her.

# Chapter Four

By MID-MORNING THE NEXT day tiny security cameras and miscellaneous paraphernalia littered Crystal's dining room table. She stood to one side and watched Cam, clipboard in hand, check off items. Tall, broad-shouldered, and narrow-hipped—he looked like he was preparing for a military campaign. His movements were efficient and purposeful.

Flutters started low in her belly. Feelings for her childhood crush had come out of hibernation and were ready to forage for food. She touched her lips with her fingertips, recalling the kiss she'd spent many sleepless nights imaging as a girl...

Apparently satisfied everything was present and accounted for, he placed the exterior cameras, flood lights, and mounting material into a leather pouch draped across his chest and hanging at waist level. With a curt nod, he buckled on his tool belt and made his way outside.

What was it about a man with a tool belt slung low on his hips that put thoughts of hot, sweaty, and naked in her mind? Following him outside, she held the ladder while he installed the first camera. The dogs lay quietly in the grass a few feet away. With him above her, she had a great view of his very nice ass.

"You must spend a lot of time working out." Crystal felt the blush creep into her cheeks and wished she had a cloak of invisibility. "Tell me you didn't hear that."

He grinned down at her. The cocky grin of the old Cam. "Well ma'am, I do aim to please."

"What made you join the Army instead of following Josh and Dave to college? I heard you turned down a sizeable scholarship." She gripped the ladder tighter as he made his way down.

Cam pulled the hem of his t-shirt up to swipe the sweat from his forehead. She hoped he hadn't caught her ogling the washboard abs he exposed. His sly grin said he had, and she blushed again.

"Simple economics really. I'd still have had room and board to cover, and Mom just didn't have the money. Student loans can be a bitch, so I looked at my options." He moved the ladder over, and she watched his biceps bunch and the muscles ripple across his back.

"And you chose the Army. Why?"

"Can't beat the GI Bill." He climbed the ladder and pulled a flood light out of his pouch. "Besides, I was eighteen and ready for adventure. See something besides a small-town Texas."

"I know you had your wild moments as a child, but you changed. From about third grade on when you started hanging with Josh." Her brows knit in confusion. "After that you seemed so responsible and focused on helping your mom."

He leveled a 'you're kidding me' look at her. "I was eighteen, and even though I would do anything for my mom… I wanted more. Dreamed about being the hero, charging to the rescue."

He climbed down, and without another word repeated the process until he'd installed three cameras—one on each corner of the house and one by the front door—and two flood lights. Crystal caught herself examining the occupant of each car that drove past and rubbed the tense muscles in her neck. Every noise made her jump—a lawn mower, kids skateboarding on the sidewalk, even the birds chirping in the trees had her searching for the source of the sound. Every time the dogs' ears twitched, she flinched.

Cam's arm settled across her back, a comforting weight. He pulled her in and soft lips brushed her cheek. She tried not to read anything into the gesture, but electricity raced down her spine.

"I know you like your life neat and predictable and safe. I wish I could make it that way for you." He scanned the equipment he'd attached to the roofline. "We'll be able to monitor any outside activity from both our computers and phones. That should give you some peace of mind.

His reassuring words brought light to the scary places. She slipped an arm around his waist and rested her head against his chest, soaking in the steadiness of the man. "I'm so glad I can count on you."

He stiffened and edged away. Folding the ladder, he tucked it under his arm. "Let's get the backyard done." She saw him wince as he stalked toward the side gate. His leg must hurt, but she'd bet he'd rather eat nails than slow down and rest for a few minutes. Why did men think they had to be invincible to be strong? Strength lay in character, and Cam was the strongest man she knew. She would trust him with her life. Shaking her head, she trailed after him and the dogs.

Just shy of two hours later, he'd installed three more cameras and two more floodlights—one camera and floodlight by the side garage door and two cameras and a floodlight on the back of her house. She'd felt safer in the backyard where she wasn't exposed to prying eyes on the street.

Finished, and glad for the chance to escape the heat, they sat at her table eating lunch while he loaded the software for the security system onto their computers and phones. With his head bent over the computer she was tempted to run her hand over his short-cropped hair and feel the soft bristle under her palm. Glancing up, he caught her inspecting him, and his dimples winked back at her. Heat crept into her cheeks.

Folding his hand over hers, Cam tugged gently. "Come on. Let me show you how this works." He spent the next fifteen minutes walking her through the program to make sure she understood what she was seeing on her computer screen and how to alert authorities if needed. "It works the same on your phone, but I'll walk you through that as well. The cameras are positioned so they only pick up activity in your yard and not your neighbors'." He grinned and laugh lines bracketed his eyes. "That's in case they ask if you're spying on them."

"I hadn't even thought about that." Were her neighbors going to think she was some kind of security nut?

"The system is set to record to the hard drive I set up in your closet and to an account I have on the cloud. I believe in redundancy." He tipped his head back and drained the last of his water. "I'm going to get the new burglar-proof locks on your windows before I head back to my place for some PT."

Her forehead wrinkled in confusion. "PT?"

"Physical Training. Gotta keep my body strong and get in my daily reps."

"You work out every day? Voluntarily?" She heard the amazement in her voice, so his chuckle wasn't entirely unexpected.

"Yes, Cro-Magnon man works out every day. If I'm ever going to make something of my life, I can't let up."

"What are you talking about?" She wanted to smack him upside the head. "Look at what you've accomplished. You're buying a house for your mom. You're starting a great new job. You're slaying dragons for me. That's a lot in my book."

"Maybe, but I let my unit down. My brothers are fighting on without me. I can't help them." His mouth thinned. He stood and grabbed his drill and a handful of locks that he stuffed in his pouch. A minute later, the sound of the bit biting into metal precluded any conversation.

Why was he shutting her out? They'd always been so close until he went away to the Army. Like a cramp in her leg she wanted to crumple and nurse the hurt. Then her spine stiffened.

She wasn't about to let him get away with that. She'd seen enough self-pity with her dad. Stomping into the guest bedroom where he stood on the bed installing a lock on the window, she halted in front of him, hands on her hips. He stopped drilling.

"And that's the crux of the problem, isn't it? You miss the life you had in the Army. You want to go back and don't think you can." She sucked in a breath. "I thought you'd planned to spend a tour in the Army and then come home to get your degree." she said. "What changed? You weren't exactly effusive in your letters."

With his back to her, he attached the lock to the window frame and said, "Originally that's what I thought. Do a tour, come home, and settle down. But in the Army, I felt like I belonged. It was family. I liked being a soldier. I had purpose." Finished, he sat on the edge of the bed, and she sat beside him with her hands folded in her lap.

She looked at the hands in her lap. "You were a soldier and to have been an Army Ranger, must have been a very good one. I'd be surprised if you didn't miss that life, but now you have the chance to be anything you want."

"I just don't know what that *anything* is. I think I'll enjoy the chance to defeat cyber criminals in the job I'll start soon, but I don't think I'm cut out to be a desk jockey." Cam huffed out a breath through his nose. "But maybe that's all I'm good for now."

"Cam, I don't believe that for a second." She watched the muscles bunch across his back.

"Could you ever have been happy with a soldier? Would that life—away from what you know and your family plus the danger—have ever been right for you?" She had to strain to hear him.

"It would have required quite an adjustment, but I don't think I would have ruled it out." She felt a flutter in her belly. As far back as high school, had Cam actually pictured them getting serious someday? That was a shock. "I would have been worried about you, knowing you were in danger and could be injured or killed. I imagine all wives and girlfriends of men in the military feel the same way and don't particularly like it, but they accept it."

He grunted and stood. "I need to finish making your place secure." When he reached her bedroom, he stopped in the doorway, an uneasy silence filled the space. She squeezed past him and followed his gaze. Walking to her bed, Crystal picked up the grey, floppy-eared, stuffed rabbit and hugged it to her chest.

"You still have Topsey?" he asked, his face an unreadable mask.

"I wouldn't be without him." She buried her nose in its matted fur. "He's seen me through a lot of sadness and heartache. Crystal looked directly at Cam. "And reminds me of the boy who never failed to stand by me."

His eyes took on a 'looking back across time' quality. "I remember the day I gave that to you." He faced her and sighed. "Your dad was in the hospital after his accident, and you looked so lost."

"And you spent the money you'd been saving to buy a bike, so you didn't have to ride double with Josh or Dave to give this and..." She slipped a finger under a chain at her throat and retrieved a silver dove pendant, "...this to me." That's the day her twelve-year-old self had fallen in puppy love with Cam.

He cleared his throat. "You needed comfort more than I needed a bike." Drill in hand he approached the window. "This and the bathroom window are my last. Then I'll take off for a few hours, but I'll leave the dogs here. That should keep Jonathan at bay if he's anywhere around."

After he'd finished and walked out the front door, the jitters returned.

It was too quiet without him, and she was too alone.

SWEAT DRIPPED DOWN HIS face, soaked his underarms, and snaked along his spine. His heart thundered, and his muscles ached. Ever since the beginning of his rehab, he'd added an extra twenty reps to each exercise in the routine his physical therapist had given him. He didn't want to lose his Ranger edge. He knew he was pushing himself, overcompensating for the damage war had done to his body.

Usually when he worked out, he was in a zone. The only thing penetrating the stillness in his mind was the clank of metal against metal or the uneven slap of his shoes on the treadmill. Today his thoughts drowned out everything else. Without a college degree, he couldn't be hired at the same level as Josh and Dave. He wasn't complaining. The Army had helped hone his computer skills to the point that he had value in the private sector, but it would take years of going to school part-time to move up in the company—if that's where he wanted to end up. *Big if.* The Army, or something in law enforcement, held appeal.

Then there was Crystal. She shouldn't settle for a broken man with modest prospects. A man whose friends got his job for him. She deserved a man who could provide the safety and security she craved. He didn't know if he could ever be that man. He still wanted to slay dragons, not quit on people like his father had. But was Cam a quitter? Other people had gone back to war after losing a limb. Did he really want to, or was he only offering lip service because he didn't think it was possible for him?

The barbell and weights settled on the rack with a decisive *clunk,* and he swiped a towel across his face as he walked into the kitchen. Opening his laptop on the counter, he checked the security feed at Crystal's. All quiet. Reaching into the cupboard he grabbed a glass, filled it with water, and chugged it down as he scanned the list of emails. He opened the one from his new employer and downloaded the forms he needed to complete before his orientation. With that, he closed his laptop and headed for the shower.

Sitting on the bathroom stool after his shower, he carefully dried his left leg stump and reattached his prosthetic. After slipping on his jeans, he stood and reached for his shirt. Shrapnel tracks, and the deep red welts running down his torso reflected back at him in the bathroom mirror. His mouth thinned. Ugly. Who would want someone like him? Damaged and defective. Quickly, he shoved his t-shirt over his head and snatched his custom-fit forearm crutches. Unless he wanted to crawl or hop—not something he wanted to do in front of Crystal—he needed them every time he removed his artificial leg. Retrieving the laptop he'd dumped on the bed, he headed out to his truck.

As soon as he pulled into Crystal's driveway, he knew something was wrong. Flowers and shards of broken glass littered her front steps. Crystal stood in the doorway, white as a sheet, a piece of paper dangling from her fingers, and the dogs alert and watchful at her heels.

# *Chapter Five*

♥

THE HINGES PROTESTED LOUDLY from the force Cam used to fling open his truck door. With a speed that surprised him, he reached her side. Gently, he removed the florist card from her icy fingers and read the note. He felt the vein pulsing at his temple.

*We're soulmates. Two halves that make a whole. Nothing will keep us apart.*

Crystal looked at him, her eyes bleak. A single tear sliced down her cheek. Sharp fragments of pain exploded like shrapnel inside him. He pulled her to him, wrapping her tightly in his arms. Her solid body—firm and real—pressing into him took the edge off the hot poker twisting in his gut... until she spoke.

"He found where I live. There's no way to escape him." Defeat laced each word. Crystal's voice tore through Cam like a blast of arctic air.

"Don't think that way. He may know where you live, but he can't control you unless you let him." Cam pressed his lips to her forehead and felt her lashes flicker against his cheek. Her hands bunched in his shirt. "I'm here to help you, but I think we should look into getting a protective order." A hard, cold lump filled his chest.

She swallowed, and he watched her jaw work with the motion. "I don't think he'll care whether or not there's a protective order, but you're right," she said. Her forehead creased, and her gaze held his. "He's unbalanced, isn't he?"

Cam wished he could lie to her. Tell her everything would be fine, but he couldn't. "Most stalkers probably have some sort of mental disorder." His mouth felt dry and he looked at the ground. "I did some research last night after you went to bed. Wanted to know what I was up against. A mental disorder doesn't necessarily mean he's dangerous." Cam looked into Crystal's blue eyes to gauge her reaction. He hoped she couldn't tell how worried he was.

Her lips thinned, and he felt her tense but was heartened to see both determination and fight in her eyes.

"Why don't you get me a broom and I'll clean this mess up," he said.

"You don't have to do that."

He held up one finger. "I want to. Let me do this for you."

She nodded and went inside.

Can pulled out his phone and watched the security feed as he walked to the side yard to get the trash bin. His scowled deepened when the video showed a car stopping at the curb and Jonathan getting out. The man opened the passenger door, retrieved a flower arrangement, and then walked to the front door. He rang the doorbell, and it looked like he planned to wait for Crystal to open the door.

Glancing at the overhead camera, Jonathan had smiled. Suddenly he started, took a step back, and placed the vase on her porch before hurrying back to his car and driving off.

Grudgingly, Cam admitted he could see why Jonathan had caught Crystal's attention. Good-looking in a pretty-boy way with blond hair, perfect smile, and dentist-whitened teeth. Cam would bet those muscles were the result of workouts with a personal trainer and maybe some steroids, instead of any real physical labor.

Crystal waited for him on the front porch, broom and dust bin in hand. He snapped a few photos of the mess and the card to send to the police before accepting the broom. "A cool drink would taste good when I'm finished here," Cam said. A shame they had to have several provable incidents before a protective order could be issued.

"I've got some iced tea in the fridge." A small smile played at her lips. "Sorry, no beer. I know how much you like it on a hot day."

She knew him so well. "Iced tea would be great."

She turned to go inside.

"Crystal?"

Glancing over her shoulder, her hand paused on the doorknob. "Hmm?"

"Have you ever had any self-defense lessons?"

Her brows shot toward her hairline and her eyes grew wide. "Do you really think it's come to that?"

He shrugged, misgiving heavy on his chest. "It wouldn't hurt. My guess is the dogs scared him off this time, but they might not always be with you." He leaned on the broom. "I could teach you a few moves." A deep chuckle rumbled from his chest. "Besides, it will give you a chance to smack me around a little." The sparkle that returned to her eyes made him feel like he'd won the lottery.

"In that case, oh Jedi Master..." She put her palms together and bowed low. "I put myself under your capable tutelage."

A half hour later, Cam found her at the dining room table leafing through a catalog. The air slowly whooshed out of the cushion as he took a seat beside her. He leaned across her arm to see what she was doing. "School classroom supplies?"

"I need to start getting ready. The school year starts in a month." She jotted down a page number on the list she was making and circled an item in the catalog.

He tipped back his glass and drained half the tea. "Are you looking forward to facing a classroom of full of kids?"

A huge grin spread across her face, and she visibly relaxed. "Can't wait. I'll be teaching first grade—my dream class—and I want everything to be perfect for them." She folded her hands and twisted to face him. "I did my student teaching with first grade. At this point, the kids haven't had a chance to form bad habits or to have heard they aren't capable, so they're eager to learn. I can't imagine anything more rewarding."

"You've always been good with kids. I remember in high school you helped with the elementary school summer program. The kids followed you around like a mother duck." He put his hand on hers and squeezed. "Changing subjects. Do you have any exercise mats?"

"Yoga mats." She cocked her head and wrinkled her nose apparently wondering where this was going.

He couldn't help himself and had to kiss that adorable nose. "I'm going to teach you some basic self-defense moves and would appreciate softening the landing." He patted her hand. "Why don't you round up those mats?

39

The living room should give us enough space. I need to collect a few things, and then I'll meet you there."

When he joined her, she was sitting on the sofa, chewing on her lip and looking like a colt ready to bolt. He cleared the magazines and decorative items off the coffee table, then hefted it and moved it into the entry. He felt her eyes on his butt and grinned. Sitting beside her, he picked up her hand and toyed with her fingers. "What's wrong?"

"Did you ever have to... hurt someone?" she asked.

"Yes." He leaned into the plush sofa cushions and stared off into a space located thousands of miles away. "I've hurt people and been responsible for deaths." He brought her hand to his lips. "It doesn't mean the violence doesn't affect you but thinking about what's at stake—your life and the lives of the people who count on you—gives you a way to accept what you have to do."

Standing, he reached out his hand to her. "Look on the bright side. You get to kick the butt you've been admiring all day." He figured that would get her going.

"I never... Why you conceited..." She stood and crossed her arms, lips set in a firm line. "Where do we start?" She bent in a wrestler stance and his lips quirked.

With a hand on each of her upper arms he positioned her in front of him. "The first thing is to recognize the vulnerable points—eyes, nose, throat, solar plexus, groin, and knees." He touched the corresponding features on his body as he listed them.

She nodded. "Got it."

"We'll start with some simple moves." He picked up his hand-held martial arts practice pads. "I'll demonstrate the straight arm thrust and then you'll pretend this pad is your target area." He thumped the middle of one pad. "The goal is to strike before your attacker gets too close. Depending on your access to nose, eyes, or throat you'll punch with the heel of your hand or your index and middle finger."

Cam executed several strikes to demonstrate each option and how to use it most effectively. "You want the force to radiate from your foot, through your hips, and into your arm. You want to fight with purpose."

Settling his hands on her hips he adjusted her stance. Awareness, like static electricity, arced from him to her and back again. He cleared his throat. "Now you try. First in slow motion aiming for the target areas, then with force into the pad."

They spent the rest of the afternoon running through a series of options—front kicks, knee to groin, and to how to free her hands. The amount of body contact increased with each new tactic.

"This is hard work." Crystal wiped the sweat from her forehead and neck with a towel.

"You're doing great. We'll finish up with what to do if you're grabbed from behind. Put your arms around me and lock your hands across my chest." Her slender arms barely reached around him, but he could feel her strength... and something else. Something deep-down satisfying that lit him like a rocket, and he had to force himself to focus.

"The object is to disorient your attacker and force him to step back. You'll lean forward as much as possible and then swing your body back, so the back of your head makes contact with his face. To keep his balance, he'll have to slide one foot forward. Quickly bend down, grab his lower leg, and then straighten up and pull his leg into your crotch. He'll fall. That's when you run." He inhaled and got a lungful of the rose shampoo she favored. "I'll walk you through the moves, and then you can try." She wiggled her hips to psych herself up. He wondered if she knew how sexy it was for her belly to cradle his butt, and he suppressed a groan.

After dumping her twice on her sweet little ass, he asked, "Are you ready to try?"

She rubbed her hands over her backside. "For payback? You bet." Pausing, she captured her bottom lip between her teeth. "What about your leg? Will you be okay?"

"My therapist has had me working out at a martial arts studio to improve my balance and maneuverability, so yeah, I'm good." Bile rose in his throat. He didn't want to be treated like an invalid.

"If you're sure..."

He nodded curtly. "First time slow, and then I'll cover my face with a pillow so you can use force."

She did the head bump slow but when she grabbed his leg, she tugged hard and he went down with a *thud*. She lost her balance and landed on top of his solar plexus. Breath rushed out of him and he gulped for air. She rolled off, but he wrapped her in his arms, twisting her until they were nose-to-nose.

White-hot heat shot from his groin and up his neck. Time stopped. He experienced an attraction so strong it flattened him like a tree in the path of a lava flow. She blinked at him, a mixture of wonder and attraction in her eyes. Those kissable lips parted, waiting—tempting him—to taste them.

Their eyes locked. His hands crept under her shirt and his thumbs skimmed the warm, creamy flesh above her waist. Her body fit his as though their contours were expressly created for each other. But she was forbidden fruit.

She arched toward him, offering what he shouldn't take. Stroking her face, he gave in to the pleasure of kissing her... a brief brush of lips before pulling back and rising awkwardly to his feet. Extending his hand, he helped her to her feet.

"I think we need to work on that move," he said. Gently he tucked a strand of hair behind her ear. "But this is enough for one day. What do you say to going out to dinner and a movie? Have some fun?"

The confusion on her face almost made him relent. She'd expected the kiss to go somewhere but his decision to keep things simple was for the best. He had to know what he was made of before he could commit.

# Chapter Six

♥

DISAPPOINTMENT NOW HAD A name and a face. Cam Rodriguez. Sitting beside him in the dark movie theater, their shoulders touching, the tantalizing smell of buttered popcorn permeating the air should have been a dream come true. Instead of enjoying the latest romantic comedy in the company of the man she'd always fantasized about, she silently fumed.

Why hadn't Cam followed through on the promise of that kiss this afternoon? She would have sworn it was leading somewhere—hopefully the bedroom. Surely he'd felt the same powerful pull of attraction that she had. But he'd stopped. Why? The sparks they'd generated would have ignited a bonfire for goodness sake. Uncertainty's claw broke loose and struck a blow.

*Maybe there was something wrong with her.*

She'd only had two serious boyfriends since high school, and they'd both fizzled out in less than a year. Maybe she just didn't have what it took to generate undying love in the opposite sex—except men like Jonathan who had a skewed understanding of love. Sighing she reached into the popcorn bucket and her fingers tangled with Cam's.

Sparks danced up her arm. His hand bounced away like he'd been zapped, scattering puffy kernels all over their laps. Peeking at him under her lashes, she studied his profile, his eyes currently riveted on the screen. He sure wasn't acting like he was unaffected. Then what was the problem? Why was he keeping her at arm's length? She thought she'd sent out signals that indicated her interest. Should she take matters into her own hands and be bold? But how exactly would she go about that? Stand around in some filmy piece of lingerie and ask if he could help her move furniture? That was so far outside her comfort zone it might as well be on Mars.

Walking back to his truck after the movie, she slipped an arm around his waist and tucked her head into his arm. He smiled at her and draped his arm across her shoulders. Companionable, but it felt like progress.

"Thanks for taking me to a girlie movie. I know you prefer car chases and tough guys, but this one made me laugh," Crystal said.

"I was hoping it would." He tugged on a loose strand of hair. "I think we both needed a break from the drama."

"I just wish I could get rid of the sensation that I'm being watched." Tilting her head, she gazed at the full moon. So peaceful. So normal. So unlike her life right now. "I'd like to strangle Jonathan for taking the enjoyment out of simple things like walking down the street or going to the grocery store. I don't like the feeling that danger might be around every corner."

Cam's lips brushed her temple and despite her unease, a thrill shimmied down her spine.

"I'm not going to let anything happen to you," he said. "For the next few weeks at least, I'm going to be your constant companion. Once we both start to work, we'll figure something out."

She could live with that and was about to tell him so when he stopped walking, tensed, and held a restraining arm across her chest. His eyes swept the parking garage, and he pushed them against a nearby car. "What the hell?"

Following his gaze, she gasped. The back window of his truck was shattered and the words, '*leave my fiancée alone*' were spray painted across the tailgate. Guilt washed over her. "Oh Cam, I'm so sorry."

"It's not your fault, so quit apologizing."

She recoiled at the harshness of his tone and he sighed. They approached his truck, and he motioned her to stay behind him while he peered in the windows. When he turned back to her the veins stood out on his neck and color tinged his cheeks. It didn't take a body language expert to realize Cam was furious.

"He left me a little present. Looks like dog shit on my back seat."

Before she had a chance to respond, her phone pinged that she had a new text message. Steeling herself, she reached into her purse and pulled out her phone. When his arms circled her, she sagged into him. With her back pressed against his chest, his cheek touching hers, she opened the message. A photo of her and Cam laughing as they walked out of the movie theater filled the screen.

Choking back an hysterical laugh, she said, "I guess it's good to know I'm not nuts. *We were being watched.*"

"Looks that way." Cam stepped away and pulled out his cell phone. Leaning against the truck, he dialed the police. In a calm voice, one she assumed he would have used during a mission, he relayed the details of the incident. When he hung up, he turned her to face him. "I heard your phone chime while I was talking to the police. What's up?"

"I don't know. I was afraid to look."

Cam held out his hand and she put her phone in it. He sat on the running board and patted the space beside him. "We'll look at it together while we wait for the police."

She wasn't sure she wanted to see what was on her phone, but Cam tugged on her hand. The thought of sitting next to him, their bodies touching from shoulder to thigh, convinced her to do as he asked.

"Ready?" he asked.

Steeling herself with a deep breath, she nodded. He tapped on the message and a selfie Jonathan had taken on their second date popped up, with the caption, *'We are so good together. How can you cheat on me?'* It was followed by a photo of them at Nate's and Lauren's wedding. She'd broken up with him soon afterwards. She'd known then there was something odd about him. Too interested in her every move. Too insistent that they spend every minute of their free time together. When he started asking her to exclude family and friends from her life and concentrate on him, she knew it was time to stop seeing him.

"I thought you said you only dated this guy a few times," Cam said as he stood, his gaze sweeping the parking area.

"I did. Three dates. Four, if you count the wedding. When my family's old insurance agent retired, Jonathan took over the business. That's how I met him. He seemed so normal. Someone I could trust." The situation made her nauseous.

Cam waved the patrol car over. After the officer took some pictures and their statements, Cam showed him the pictures and messages sent by Jonathan. "Now that we have more than one incident we can connect to Jonathan,

Crystal will contact her attorney this evening about getting a protective order. Is there anything else we should do?"

"Continue keeping records of all calls, emails, or other contact, and get copies to us." The officer flipped his clip board shut and motioned at Cam's truck. "Unless there is something on the garage security camera, which I doubt, we don't have enough proof to charge Mr. Small with the damage done to your vehicle."

The two men shook hands and once the patrol car left Cam disposed of the poop and swept away as much glass as he could. "That's about the best I can do without soap and water and a vacuum. Let's get out of here."

Crystal wrung her hands and felt like she'd stepped out of a sauna, drained and limp. This was all her fault. They drove with the windows down to alleviate the smell. Luckily Texas summer nights were warm.

When they arrived at Crystal's, Cam checked the interior security footage on his phone before they went in. Dropping her purse on the kitchen counter, Crystal turned to Cam. "Up until we reached your truck, I had a lovely time." She rubbed her eyes with the heel of her hand. "I'm exhausted. I'm going to bed." She wasn't lying. She had about as much energy as a rock. Even the temptation of spending time with Cam didn't arouse any enthusiasm.

·♥·♥·♥·♥·♥·

CAM PUNCHED HIS PILLOW and shifted again, trying to get comfortable. Plucking his phone off the end table, he looked at the time and discovered he'd been tossing and turning for over two hours. He hoped Crystal was getting more sleep than he was. The way Jonathan had looked in the camera when he delivered the flowers, and the boldness with which he sent images and messages to Crystal, told Cam the man didn't care who knew what he was up to.

Goose bumps rose on his arms, bringing to mind that old saying, 'someone is walking across your grave.' A scream pierced the silence and his heart stopped. The dog in his room whined. In one motion Cam swung his legs over the bed, grabbed his crutches and gun, and was in Crystal's room in fifteen seconds flat.

She was sitting up in bed disoriented and sobbing. The two dogs he'd left in her room whimpered but their tails thumped against the carpet, so an intruder in the house didn't seem likely. In the split second it took for his brain to assess the situation, he made his way to her bed. Setting his gun on the bedside table, he rocked her in his arms, stroked her hair, and crooned, "It's alright, Baby. I'm here. Nothing will hurt you."

Gradually the sobbing and shaking subsided. Crystal swiped at her cheeks and drew in a shaky breath. "I'm sorry. I didn't mean to disturb you."

"You didn't. I wasn't asleep. What happened? Did you hear something?" He cupped her face in his hands. So soft. She smelled fresh like the air after a rainstorm. His body clenched at the nearness, the intimacy of holding her in nothing but her silky tap pants and teddy against his bare chest. She buried her face in his neck and his arms slipped around her so he could rub her back.

"No, my old nightmare returned." He felt her lips move against his neck and desire pooled in his crotch.

"The one where you relive your dad's accident?" His chest ached at her pain.

She nodded. "It's all so vivid. I can feel the rain in my hair and my wet clothing plastered to my body. The line shack where I planned to wait out the storm. The crack of lightening, the horse rearing, my dad hitting the ground. He was so still."

She shuddered, and he pulled her closer. "You kept your head and handled it well. Only twelve, and you called for help and then rendered first aid."

"But..." she started.

He silenced her with a finger across her lips. "What happened was not your fault." He meant the kiss to be one of comfort, but she had other ideas. She deepened the kiss, and when her fingers scraped down his back, passion took over. The blood pounding in his ears blocked the voice telling him he shouldn't do this. If she offered herself, a kiss wouldn't be enough. He wanted to bury himself inside of her. He wanted to go to paradise and back with her.

When she lifted the teddy over her head and dropped it to the floor, he was a goner. The soft mounds of her breasts, bathed in the dim light spilling from the hallway, took his breath away.

"Are you sure?"

In response, she laced her fingers behind his head and opened her mouth to him. Her breasts pressed into his chest. Trailing kisses down her neck and chest, he reached his goal and took one of her nipples in his mouth, teasing it with his tongue.

Moaning, she arched to give him better access. She was heaven, and everything inside him soared. Her fingers skimmed his side and when they traced over his scars, he flinched and drew back. He was broken, and she was perfect.

Her hands framed his face. "I know about your scars." Her eyes bore into him with an unexpected intensity. "Your wounds are part of you. Part of the man I..." She swallowed, "Respect and care about. You're beautiful." She bent her head and kissed each scar from his ribs to his thigh removing his boxers in the process.

With her tender touches and kisses, she burst the dam of humiliation and shame he felt about her seeing his wounds. He hadn't been intimate with anyone since he'd lost his leg. Afraid of the look of disgust he'd find on his partner's face. Crystal didn't care. When she reached the stub of his leg and gently caressed the puckered skin with her lips, he closed his eyes and let the emotion pour through him like hot oil. She took him to heights he had no idea he could reach.

He splayed his hands and ran them down her back tracing each ridge and valley along the way. She was so soft, his hands glided across her skin. Gently grasping her upper arms, he eased her onto her back. He wanted to drink her in, feast on those luscious lips, lavish praise on her perfect breasts, and in general, worship her body in the way this amazing woman deserved.

Her eyes sparkled with a devotion that halted the breath in his chest. He may not be worthy of her, but he couldn't deny she seemed to see something in him that made him pause and wonder... could they have a chance? Her eyelids fluttered closed, and he touched his lips to that delicate skin. From there he followed the line of her brow to her temple and down her hairline to her ear. His tongue traced the sensitive spot below her lobe. The erotic hum she made drove him wild.

With feather-light pressure he dragged his lips over her neck and chest until he had one turgid nipple in his mouth. As he suckled, she bucked.

"Oh, Cam. Now. Now." Her breath came in short bursts and her fingers scraped his back.

"Not yet Baby, but soon. I have a few more places I want to explore, first." His erection throbbed, but he wasn't ready for this to end. He wanted their first time together to create memories that would last them a lifetime.

She writhed beneath him. "I'm going to die if you aren't inside me soon. Explore all you want later."

"Patience grasshopper. You still have much to learn." And he proceeded to teach her just how much.

He pressed wet, open-mouthed kisses along her abdomen, over her hips, and down her inner thigh. His fingers found her nub and worked their magic until her core was wet and hot and her body covered in a thin film of sweat. The scent of sex permeated his senses. He inserted one finger and added another as her body stretched to accommodate them and teased that tender bud deep within.

When her walls contracted and she moaned in release, he was grateful he could give her such pleasure. Easing back, he kissed her navel and then rose on an elbow to look in her eyes. Regret pounded him like an 800-pound gorilla. "I don't have a condom with me."

"I do." She reached into the bedside table and pulled out a shiny, gold packet.

"You're a goddess." He wasn't going to ask why she had a condom handy, but he felt a pinch near his heart.

"I bought the box on a whim. Have no idea why, but sure am glad I did." She smiled at him and nipped his chin. "Now let's put it to good use."

She'd read his mind. Happiness was probably oozing out his pores in flashes of crackling light. He thrust into her, and they rocked together in perfect harmony as though they'd known each other in another life. His balls tightened, happiness exploded into ecstasy, and his love spilled out of him.

Making love to Crystal wouldn't be a one-time affair. No matter how wrong he was for her, he'd cling to this until she saw the truth and moved on. He wasn't the man she needed, but he would give her everything that he could. "Caramel," he whispered as she settled into his embrace and her breathing evened.

# *Chapter Seven*

CAM WOKE WITH CRYSTAL'S butt snuggled into his groin, the smell of her floral shampoo in his nose, and a decided hard-on urging him to pick up where they'd left off last night. Instead, he rolled out of bed, careful not to disturb her, slipped his arms through his crutch's cuff, and left the room with the dogs at his heels. Having breakfast ready for her when she woke sounded like the gentlemanly thing to do. Romantic and thoughtful.

He knew the minute she stepped into the kitchen. Looking over his shoulder, he smiled at her. Her expression held a mixture of shyness and uncertainty. She paused in the doorway, one foot on top of the other. Finding a new rhythm the morning after wasn't something he had a lot of experience with and guessed she didn't either. The question of 'where do we go from here' circled above their heads.

She sniffed. "Bacon and pancakes?" Moving into the room she peeked around his shoulder and looked into the skillet. "And mushroom and tomato omelet?"

"I took a chance that this was still your favorite breakfast. Luckily you had all the ingredients." Cam felt inordinately pleased with himself when her lips brushed his cheek.

"You remembered right."

He loved her bashful smile. It reminded him of a youthful, carefree world that held nothing but promise. "Pour yourself some coffee and grab some plates. I don't know about you, but I'm starving."

"Did you get all your school supplies ordered?" he asked after they'd loaded their plates and sat down. He didn't want to break the spell by talking about what their day's agenda really held—scrubbing and deodorizing his truck, getting the back window replaced, and following up with the attorney about the status of the protective order. Plenty of time for all of that later.

"I did. The box should arrive tomorrow. Can't wait to see it all in the classroom." She slipped a bite of omelet in her mouth and closed her eyes. The sound she made had blood rushing south of his belt buckle, and he almost groaned.

Clearing his throat he said, "I'd be happy to help. Carry the boxes, climb on the stepladder, push in the thumbtacks, clean the chalkboard."

"I'd love your company." She blushed but then her face fell. "Are you worried about me being alone?"

His heart did a nosedive. "Partly, and partly I like helping you." He wiped his mouth with his napkin giving the tightness in his chest a chance to ease. "Let's enjoy our breakfast before we open the door to reality too wide."

She swallowed and nodded. "Works for me. So, how's your mom? Excited about her new house?"

Pride had him swelling like a puffer fish. "She's like a kid in a candy store. My inbox is filled with photos of furniture, rugs, and paint colors. She's over the moon about being a first-time homeowner." He shrugged. "Not that I can help her decide between Queen Anne and French Country or pale sage and Magnolia blossoms. Its furniture and paint." He couldn't contain the chuckle. "She needs a daughter for this duty."

"I see her more as the practical yet charming French Country style and the brightness of Magnolia Blossoms on the walls." She scrunched her nose. "Your mom is just not the formality and fussiness of Queen Anne."

"I'll take your word for it. Just give me a recliner and a big screen television and I'm a happy camper."

Crystal rolled her eyes, and he couldn't resist leaning over and brushing his lips over hers. She tasted of maple syrup and coffee. "You can tell her that when we see her at your dad's big birthday bash next weekend." He sighed and sat back. If only all of this were happening a few years from now. After he had his degree and better job prospects. The leg situation wouldn't change, but at least he'd be in a better position to support a family for the long haul.

Pushing away from the table, he stood. "I guess I've put off dealing with my truck long enough. Time to face the mess. Point me toward a vacuum and a bucket and scrub brush and I'll get started."

He followed her to the laundry room, the dogs' nails clicking on the wood floor. She opened a cupboard and handed him a brush, a bottle of carpet cleaner, several soft cloths, and a bottle of commercial leather cleaner.

"The bucket and Shop-Vac are in the garage. I'll clean up the dishes and be out to help in a few minutes," she said. "What are you going to do about the spray paint?"

"Took care of it last night after you went to bed while it could still be removed with soap and water."

Standing in the darkened garage, Cam called a mobile auto glass repair place and arranged to have his back window replaced. He pushed the garage door opener button and listened to the clicking of the chain as it moved through the gears.

Handwritten posterboard signs, tacked to wooden stakes, lined the edge of the lawn by the sidewalk. '*You're mine. I love you. Don't leave me. We belong together.*'

Jonathan. Anger churned its way through his gut.

He'd obviously stayed on the sidewalk and not come near the house or the dogs would have alerted him. The guy seemed to be unraveling. Cam's eyes swept the street checking to see if Jonathan was anywhere in the vicinity. He wasn't, but several neighbors stood in their yards, whispering among themselves.

Cam raised his hand in greeting, smiled, and hoped to put their minds at rest that everything was under control. Nothing to see here. The neighbors quickly turned and went back inside. Great. Nothing like having a psycho decorating your lawn to make a good impression. Snapping a few pictures for the record, he started to remove the signs before Crystal saw them. He was too late, and her gasp from the front porch tore at his heart.

"Oh my God," she said. "How? When?"

She came up beside him and her fingers dug into his bicep. Prying her fingers loose, he pulled her into his arms and kissed the top of her head. She trembled, and a murderous rage rose in his throat. "I'm sorry you had to see this. I'd hoped to get them out of sight." What he wouldn't give to corral Jonathan in a dark, deserted alley.

A tear trickled down her cheek, but she shook her head. "I know you want to protect me, but I have to face the ugly as well as the good." She glanced over the expanse of grass and shuddered. "From the time I was little you told me I was strong. I need to start living up to your claim." Stepping out of his arms, she squared her shoulders. "You've already taken a picture for the police?" she asked.

He blew a breath out through his lips. "Yeah, I took a photo and now I'm going to check the security feed. Hopefully we caught him on camera." He pulled out his phone. Her hair swept over his arm as she leaned around him to see. On the screen, a man in jeans and a hoodie walked into range, carrying the signs, which he stuck in the grass as he walked along the sidewalk. He halted, took a photo, and then retraced his steps until he was out of sight. He kept his head down and face hidden.

Kicking one of the signs, Crystal said, "I suggest we dump these in the trash where they belong." She blew out a frustrated breath. "Though I suppose we should check with the police first to make sure they don't need them."

They'd just finished putting the offending reminders of Jonathan's obsession in the side yard when the glazier arrived. Crystal rolled the Shop-Vac over to Cam's truck and started vacuuming the back seat and floor while Cam dealt with the repairman. A stab of guilt pierced Cam's heart. She didn't need to do his dirty work. This was a job for grunts like him not angels like her. As soon as he got the glass situation squared away, Cam grabbed the bucket, filled it with water, and joined Crystal. They worked in silence until they'd scoured every inch.

After paying the auto glass repairman, they stood in the driveway and watched him drive down the street. "Now that the truck is sealed again, I can set off a deodorizing bomb and hopefully get rid of the smell. We'll need to stick around until it's finished because the air conditioner needs to run." He pulled two folding chairs off a peg in the garage and set them in the shade under the tree. "Sit with me?"

"Okay." She swiveled to face him once he'd set off the canister and lowered himself into the other chair. "Again, I am so sorry about all of this. Your brand-new truck."

"Is that what's been eating you? It's just a truck. Don't worry about it." His body felt like he'd consumed too much caffeine. He inhaled and plunged ahead. "I was afraid you regretted last night." He studied a bare spot in the grass where the tree roots ran along the surface.

"No. Not at all. How could you think that?"

He watched her eyes shift and braced for the '*but we can't ever do that again*' he was afraid was coming.

She grimaced. "Truth. I'm a little embarrassed. I'm still that kid who's afraid there's a monster under my bed and just want to pull the covers over my head and hide."

Relief poured over him like a gentle rain. "Ah Caramel." He smoothed a hand down her hair. "We all have monsters under our beds and we all need help fighting them off. I'm glad I could be there for you. But I was really talking about what happened *after* the nightmare. Are you sure there're no regrets?"

"Of all the things in my life I could regret, last night, making love to you, isn't one of them. I could never regret you."

"As long as you're sure. I never want to hurt you." What he was doing might be wrong, but if it helped her cope, he'd man up and give her what she needed to get through this. He just had to banish long-term from his mind.

"Positive."

"And by the way, given the circumstances, wanting to hide—not so unusual." He squeezed her hand. "I'm impressed by how well you're holding up." He curled his fingers into hers, feeling her softness against his callused palms.

She offered up a wobbly smile and then asked, "What's the game plan once your truck is finished cooking?"

She started and put a hand over her heart when her phone chimed.

"Want me to look at it first?" Cam asked.

"Together maybe?"

Scooting his chair closer until the metal armrests scraped, he held out his hand. Her hand trembled as she turned the phone over to him. He wanted to rub the knot forming in his neck but showing tension might increase hers. They could see the text was from Jonathan. Anger clouded his vision, but he managed to open the attachment.

'*Like my artwork? It's all for you. I miss you. We have to be together.*' The accompanying image showed her front lawn lined by the signage.

"What is wrong with that man?" Crystal asked shifting to face Cam.

Cam let out a breath he hadn't realized he was holding. It felt good to see the flash of spirit in her eyes. The fighter he'd known as a child was still in there. She might try to deny its existence, but she'd battled lots of hardship and won.

"Jonathan is really pissing me off," he said as he got up to turn off the truck's motor.

"What's the verdict?" she asked when he rejoined her.

"Much better, but we may want to drive with the windows down for a while." Her phone rang as he sat back down. She glanced at the caller ID and picked up. When she disconnected, he asked, "Your attorney?"

"The judge turned down the request for a protective order—didn't think the actions were threatening—but did issue a warrant for harassment. He said the police will pick Jonathan up and he'll be in jail long enough for them to process the paperwork. After that, he'll most likely be released on bail. The police will give Jonathan a stern warning that any continued harassment will not be viewed kindly by the courts." She covered her face with her hands and put her head on her knees. "Oh god, what if I've made everything worse?"

Cam rubbed her back. "No honey, you did the right thing. I'm sure he'll back off after this. He's a businessman with a reputation to protect." The sinking feeling in Cam's gut mocked his reassuring words.

She sat up and looked him in the eye. She wasn't buying the lie.

"Tell you what," he said. "I think we need a break. After we stop by the police station and report this latest incident, why don't we go visit your parents? A day on the ranch would do us both some good, and even if Jonathan follows us, he won't be able to get close enough to the house to cause trouble without someone spotting him." He nudged her shoulder with his. "Maybe we could go out to the old swimming hole. Just the two of us?" Her smile warmed him all the way to his toes.

"But don't you have other things you need to be doing? Like maybe help your mom pack?"

"Nope. Mom has a bunch of friends who've volunteered to help her." He scratched the head of the dog nearest him. "The dogs will love the chance to get out and run."

"Okay then. I'll give my folks a call and tell them we'll be there in a few hours." She bounced up and made a beeline for the front door with two of the dogs at her heels.

He watched the sway of her hips as she walked away, and a grim determination settled in his chest. He would protect her at all costs.

# Chapter Eight

♥

THE WIND RUSHED THROUGH the open windows of the truck, the heated air mingling with the air conditioner. Crystal had told Cam that she didn't mind the heat, but he'd insisted on doing what he could to make her comfortable. The dogs, in the back seat of the extended cab, must have thought they'd died and gone to heaven. Their ears flapped in the wind, and their noses pointed to the sky sucking in every scent they could.

They'd spotted an SUV they thought was Jonathan's following them a few car-lengths back on the interstate. Crystal's stomach clenched at the possibility of a confrontation. When they turned off onto the two-lane country road that passed by her parent's ranch, the other vehicle did, too, but kept its distance.

Cam put his hand over hers on the console and squeezed, his smile warm and reassuring. "There's nothing we can do. If he's stupid enough to follow us on to the ranch, we'll have his ass hauled in for trespassing." He paused a beat and she watched a sly smile tug at his lips. "That is if someone doesn't shoot him first. Personally, I vote for option number two."

"I don't want to see anyone get hurt. I just want it to stop." She pressed her fist to her chest and rubbed in a circular motion to ease the tight spot behind her sternum.

"I know you don't, but I want to make sure you're safe. Drastic action may be the only way to do that." He squeezed her hand again, then turned onto the ranch's gravel entrance road. Stopping, he reached out and punched the new code into the gate's keypad. The electric motor whirred, and the gate swung open.

Cam glanced in the rearview mirror as the SUV stayed on the country road. "Jonathan's behind the wheel, but he's not trying to follow us."

Crystal made a show of swiping her hand across her forehead. "Whew. I'm not in the mood for a fight." She rested her arm on the open window and gazed across the acres of feed corn her dad had planted in the pastures on either side of the gravel drive. Two miles down the road, they reached the house. Her dad, mom, and brother lounged on the front porch sipping lemonade. They raised their glasses in salute as Cam pulled to a stop.

"That looks mighty good," Cam said stepping onto the porch. Pulling her brother, Wayne, into a bro hug, he slapped him on the back. "Hear you've got your veterinary license. Congrats, man."

"Thanks." Her tall brother ducked his head but grinned showing off the Kincaid dimples. Wayne ruffled his sister's hair. "I'm sure Crystal told you I joined Nate's practice."

"She did. Looks like it agrees with you." Cam stepped over and hugged Crystal's mom. "Jessalyn, you're pretty as ever. Are you enjoying your summer vacation? Those high school students treating you alright?"

Crystal grinned when her mom blushed. Cam may think his wounds impacted his appeal but every woman he came in contact with proved him wrong.

"Yes, to both questions. I may be tiny, but the kids know I have every single one of their parents on speed dial." Her soft laughter swirled around them like a balm.

"Mom, have you done something different to your hair?" Crystal asked.

Jessalyn eyed the two men in her life who had the good sense to appear chastised. "At least someone noticed." She fluffed her chin-length, fawn-colored hair. "I had it layered a little and some highlights added."

"Looks good." Crystal kissed her mom on the cheek.

Cam leaned down to her dad in his wheelchair and gripped Harry's hand. "Hey Harry. The ranch looks great. I see you've made those improvements to the barn I heard about."

"I did. While the women folk are getting our lunch ready... and gossiping about us... I'll give you a tour." He glanced over at his son. "Wayne here promised to vaccinate our new foals, and I need to supervise." He winked at his son.

Crystal did a double take and pursed her lips. Was that her dad teasing and smiling? She'd seen small changes in his attitude over the past year, but this was a major breakthrough. What was that about?

Jessalyn steered her daughter toward the door and made a shooing motion with her other hand. "You men go on and finish your chores. Lunch is noon sharp. If you're late, you go without."

·♥·♥·♥·♥·♥·

WAYNE STOPPED BY HIS truck to pick up his supplies while Cam followed Harry to the barn. He stepped forward to open the door. "No, wait," Harry said. Pulling a remote out of his wheelchair bag, he pressed a button. The door slid open. "Solar-powered electric motor with a battery backup."

The man's pleased smile warmed Cam's heart. "That's quite a gadget you've got there. Let me see." Harry handed the remote over and Cam closed and opened the door. "This must make your life a lot easier."

"It does. I don't need to wait for someone else to open it. I've made a lot of changes these past few years that let me take a more active role in running the ranch."

Wayne walked by. "I'll get those foals taken care of."

"You go ahead. I'm going to show Cam what I've done." Harry wheeled down the center aisle and out the other end, talking as he went. "I extended the barn another thirty-five feet, adding five stalls and a vet room. I've turned out top cutting horses in the past, so I built on that to expand our operation to include a full-fledged breeding and training program. Here's our new vet room." He waved to Wayne as he rolled by and out into the yard. "New hot walker. New paddocks." He rolled up to the pipe fencing and angled his chin indicating a ramp that led to a platform perched above the fence. "From there I can oversee training." He rested his arms on one of the rails and peered into the training arena. "Like I said, lots of changes."

"Hopefully Crystal will stop worrying. The changes look good on you." Cam folded his arms across his chest and gazed into the arena.

"I know. I need to have a talk with her." Cam felt Harry's gaze bore through him like a drill. "There were a lot of years I gave her cause for concern. I pretty much wallowed in self-pity and doubt." He gripped Cam's arm. "Don't make the same mistakes I did. You've got a lot going for you. Your health, a good job, family and friends that love you... and my daughter gets stars in her eyes when she looks at you. I had all that and pissed it away by shutting out the people who loved me." A faraway look entered his eyes. "Truth? I think I did it to punish myself for the loser I thought I was. It took forever to win it all back."

"I wish what you said is true, but I'm not the same man anymore." Cam ran a hand over his short-cropped hair. "I used to be a warrior. I was tough. I took care of people." He drew in a deep breath. "Now? Who knows?" His hands balled into fists at his side, and his shoulders ached with the strain.

"Nope, you're not the same man and your life *has changed*." Harry looked off into the distance and his voice drifted back to Cam. "It's up to you whether you're better or worse. You can let your experience give you new insights and strength or you can let it send you to the bottom of the ocean... no light, no air. Only a pressure that will crush you." Harry wheeled his chair around to face Cam. "You're still a warrior, so fight this. You'll never know what you're capable of until you try. Remember failure is not defeat. Giving up is."

Cam nodded, his throat too tight for words. If other people believed in him, could he believe in himself?

Harry patted Cam's arm. "Think about it." He pivoted his chair and headed for the barn. "Let's get in out of the sun." They'd progressed a few feet when Harry said, "I hear you've been teaching Crystal self-defense. You think Jonathan might still come after her now that you've alerted the police?"

Cam relayed what had transpired over the past twenty-four hours as they re-entered the barn. The retelling had the anger, fear, and frustration slamming into him with the force of the IED that took out his leg.

"Shit," Harry said. "I'm glad you're with her. I trust you to take care of her."

"I'll do my best, sir." God, he hoped he was up to the task.

"I hear you two are heading out to the swimming hole after lunch." Harry narrowed his eyes. "Are you armed?"

"Yes Sir. Got my Glock and Beretta with me and extra clips. Plus the dogs." He scratched the head of the German Shepard mix sitting beside him.

"You're welcome to take one of my shotguns with you. Never can tell when you might run across a varmint that needs exterminating."

Cam barked out a laugh and clapped Harry on the shoulder. "Thanks for the offer, but I think I'm covered. Don't want to make the firepower too obvious and scare Crystal."

"Good point," Harry said. "That girl has worked real hard to convince herself that she should be afraid of her own shadow." He raised his hand in greeting as Crystal entered the barn. "Hi, sweetheart. How's lunch coming?"

She tucked her hand into Cam's and bent to kiss her dad on the cheek. "You know Mom. Everything is under control."

Cam glanced up at the sound of a stall door opening. Wayne stepped out and walked toward them. "I just got a call from Zach, and he'd like me to run over and take a look at a brood mare he's thinking of buying." He lifted his ball cap and slicked back his dark brown hair. "Jeez, it's hotter than a two-dollar pistol today." He replaced his cap. "I'll be back before lunch is served." He looked at Cam. "Want to come?"

Cam squeezed Crystal's hand. "Do you mind?"

"No, you two go on," she said. "It'll give me a chance to catch up with Dad."

He brushed his lips against her temple and followed Wayne to his truck.

·♥·♥·♥·♥·♥·

HER DAD TOOK HER hand and stroked it like he had when she was little. The soothing act tumbled her back across the years to a time when her dad was the man who made everything right. This was the man she'd yearned to return ever since the accident.

"How are you holding up?" he asked. "Cam told me about his truck and the other things Jonathan has done in the last few days. Not gonna lie. It worries me."

His brows pulled together and she recognized that determined set to his shoulders... a posture she hadn't seen in far too long. It was like her dad of old had finally found his way back home. Her body stilled, wondering if the changes she'd witnessed were real or imagined.

"Cam's kept me steady. Providence must have put him in my path at this exact right moment." She flutter-patted her chest to contain the fullness in her heart. She was one lucky lady.

"I'm glad he's with you. He's a good man and I trust him." Harry clasped his hands in his laps and looked into the shadows of the barn. "I figure the past few months have been hard on you. Making all these changes because of Jonathan. Moving. Changing your phone and email. Always looking over your shoulder." A small smile bloomed on his lips. "You're not big on change, but I'm proud of how well you're standing up to all of this. Shouldn't be surprised though. You've always risen to the occasion."

"Do you really think so?" She felt the need to sit down. Praise from her dad?

"Yes, I do." Her dad's voice was strong and clear. "It's high time you realized it."

Swallowing hard she said, "Mom told me about all the improvements you've made to the place in the last year. I can't believe I didn't notice before this."

"You had your own life." He wheeled himself over to a bench along the wall. "Take a load off. My neck's getting a crick in it staring up at you."

"I'm sorry. I should have thought," she said grimacing.

Her dad rolled his eyes. "Don't be. I'm joshing you. Now sit. I'd like to catch up."

Crystal sank onto the wooden bench and leaned her back against the rough wood of the barn wall, feeling the pull of splinters on her knit top. "I still should have noticed all the changes... including you. You're different, Dad."

"To be fair, your visits these last few years have been infrequent." He patted her knee. "What with growing up, that's to be expected." His gaze dropped. "And I know I wasn't always a joy to be around." When he looked up and into her eyes, she felt a jolt. "I also know you felt responsible for my accident and that's on me. I'm sorry."

Pain circled her heart attacking like a virus consuming its host. Words squeezed past the lump in her throat. "If I hadn't run off in a snit, you wouldn't have been out there. You would have been safe at home."

"That's where you're wrong." His voice sounded like someone dragging an old tire over gravel. "My accident was a perfect storm. I'd had a fight with your mom about her going back to teaching instead of staying home to help me on the ranch. I'd had too much to drink. I acted like the pigheaded, stubborn man I was and stormed off. I shouldn't have been on a horse riding around like a maniac." He looked at the ceiling and she watched his Adam's apple bob as he swallowed.

A huge crack opened in her heart and tears pooled in her eyes. "But you were out there looking for me, and that's on me."

He shook his head sadly. "I was out there but not for you. You're a ranch kid. I knew you'd be fine. Damn fool that I am, I wanted to hurt your mom. Whether or not you'd run off, I'd have been out there." He framed her face with his hands and swiped her tears with his thumbs. "I should never have allowed you to keep carrying this guilt. I was angry for such a long time... not at you, never at you. You saved my life." He put his hands back in his lap and studied them. "I was angry at myself. Angry at my situation. Angry I wasn't much of a man anymore." His sigh came from the depths of his soul. "None of that was your fault. It took your mom telling me to either get some help with an attitude adjustment or she was leaving."

Crystal sucked in a quick breath and thought her heart might have stopped. "Oh my God. I had no idea you and mom were having problems." She placed her hand on his arm and he patted it.

"Turns out that was the kick in the butt I needed. Joined a support group and realized what a jackass I'd been. Started focusing on all the things I could do, and that turned out to be a pretty long list."

She leaned over and hugged him, breathing in the hay and honest sweat that characterized the Dad of her youth. "You are one of the most remarkable, inspiring people I know. I'm glad I'm your daughter."

Harry cleared his throat and color crept up his neck. "Enough of that." They glanced toward the open barn door at the sound of a truck pulling into the yard.

Her mom's voice floated in. "You boys go wash up. I'm going to get your dad and Crystal. Lunch is ready."

A few seconds later, Jessalyn's slim frame was silhouetted in the doorway. Her dad's face split in a huge grin and Crystal felt lighter than she had in years. While she couldn't rid herself of all the old ghosts with one conversation, chunks of the fear and guilt she'd been carrying around crumbled into dust and settled at her feet.

# Chapter Nine

♥

JONATHAN FOLLOWED CRYSTAL AND *'that guy'*—that's who Cam was in his mind—to the entrance road to her parent's ranch. He kept driving, delighted they were going here instead of her uncle's ranch. As the person who had taken over insuring their property when he bought out their retiring insurance agent's business, Jonathan knew the layout well. Not only had he toured the property to update their policy, he also had a topographic map of the ranch. But for all his hard work, they'd fired him. Fired him—and simply due to a misunderstanding he'd had with Crystal.

Two miles down the road, he turned off on one of the many access roads into the Kincaid's ranch. There was a gate with only a chain to keep it closed. No locks. This time of year, the cattle were in the summer pastures on the far side of the ranch so no one visited this section unless a fence was reported down. He drove in a few miles and parked beside the line shack that served to protect ranch hands from the elements when necessary.

Dressed in loose-fitting camouflage cargo pants, a light tan cotton t-shirt, a camouflage ball cap, and running shoes, Jonathan stepped out of his BMW SUV. Slinging a backpack containing binoculars, topographic map, a camera, water, and snacks over his shoulders; he set off at a steady jog. Time for all those hours spent with a personal trainer to pay off. He figured he could cover the two miles in about twenty minutes. On a previous visit he'd scouted out a bluff overlooking the ranch compound. The location offered a great vantage point to see what was happening and had enough vegetation to prevent detection.

When he reached his destination, he pulled out his binoculars and lay down. Everyone was gathered on the front porch back-slapping and hugging and looked to be enjoying an easy camaraderie. Jonathan seethed that he hadn't been accepted as readily. So what if Cam was an old family friend. Yeah, he knew the history. Small town. Word got around. Jonathan was the better man—not some defective has-been—and should have been accorded greater respect.

Crystal and her mom disappeared into the house and the men into the barn. Later, Wayne and Cam took off in his truck but returned shortly before noon. Not much to see, so Jonathan fanaticized what it would be like when he and Crystal were married. She'd love him unconditionally. Look at him with adoring eyes. Cater to his every whim. And the sex... would be hot. He got hard just thinking about her lush body under his total control.

When the family came out of the house after lunch, he assumed Cam and Crystal would return to Austin, so he started gathering up his stuff for the hike back to his SUV. His hand stalled as they climbed into one of the John Deere Gators—a small, all-terrain, mini truck that Harry used to get around and oversee the work of the ranch hands. From the towels and blankets tossed in the bed of the Gator, he guessed their destination was somewhere along the river that cut through the property. Cam motioned, and the dogs hopped in the back.

A white-hot heat roared through his system. His hands clenched and unclenched. No telling what Cam would do to her, alone, frolicking in the water. Jonathan couldn't stand the thought of another man's hands on her. Touching what belonged to him. He couldn't follow them on foot. He needed another mode of transportation. Something that couldn't be easily detected but would give him the speed he needed to keep up. His mountain bike. He could stash it in the line shack, and even if by some remote chance someone discovered it, they wouldn't know whose it was or how it got there. He'd do it this week before the big birthday bash for Harry next weekend. He knew Crystal would be there, and he'd heard Cam and his mom had been invited as well. If Crystal and Cam snuck off during the event, he'd be able to follow to see what they were up to.

Plans made, a cold calm settled over him. A man had to protect what belonged to him.

·❤ · ❤ · ❤·❤·❤·

THE NEXT MORNING, CRYSTAL sighed as complete contentment filtered through her like water seeping through pebbles in a jar. Yesterday afternoon by the river had been perfect. She rose on her elbow and gazed at the man sleeping beside her. His strong jaw was relaxed in sleep and a dark shadow of stubble outlined his chiseled cheeks. Tempted to trail her fingertips over his powerful chest and defined abs, she resisted the urge, not wanting to wake him. The man needed his rest after yesterday's exertions by the river and again in her bed last night. A small smile played around her well-kissed lips. She could get used to this. Cam was the complete package. Tough and resourceful yet compassionate and tender. He stirred and turned his head, sleepy bedroom eyes shooting heat through her veins.

"Good morning," he said his voice morning raspy. "Sleep well?" His fingers tangled in her hair as he drew her to him for a kiss. "What's on today's agenda?"

Lazing around with you all day sounds good." Her fingers slid along his cheek savoring the pull of his beard. Sharp prickles that spoke of intimacy. Flopping on her back she sighed. "At some point I need to visit my classroom and start organizing it for the students." Excitement tingled in her stomach. *Her classroom. Her students.*

"I'll help with that. Maybe we could do it this morning? I need to stop by work this afternoon for my orientation session with HR." He stretched his arms over his head and she wanted to run her tongue along those rippling muscles. "I can't believe we both start work in just a few weeks."

"So much for lazing around." She sat up and moved to get out of bed. His arm snaked around her waist and his lips pressed against the indentation at the base of her spine. A jolt of electricity shot straight to her core, making her moist and panting to feel him inside her.

He trailed kisses up her back. "I know we need to get up, but I think we should share a shower. Conserve water and all." His voice was a husky whisper against her ear, sending another shiver of desire into her most feminine parts.

"You had me at sharing a shower." She stood and rolled her shoulders.

He swiveled toward his side of the bed scooting until his good leg dangled over the edge, grabbed his crutches, and made his way toward the bathroom. Doubt stilled her feet. How was this supposed to work? Standing on one leg in a slippery shower and making love sounded like a recipe for disaster.

Glancing over his shoulder, he grinned. "Coming?"

She made a show of removing her camisole and tap pants, enjoying the way his eyes darkened. "You bet." She couldn't let him see her concern and risk wounding his pride. They'd figure it out. They just might have to get a little creative. Following him into the bathroom, he already had the shower going and was unfolding a small, plastic stool with rubber suction cups on its legs. Apparently, he was way ahead of her.

"I never saw that before," she said running her finger down his spine and feeling the muscles contract under her touch. He rewarded her by hauling her into his arms and kissing her until her bones liquefied. The man could rent out those lips and make a fortune.

His breath mingled with hers as he spoke. "I figured I'd be spending a lot of time here so decided to bring in a few essentials." He put his hand under the spray to test the temperature then pushed his boxers to the floor.

Drool collected in her mouth at the sight of all that sculpted flesh. Broad chest, nipples she wanted to run her tongue over, washboard abs, and those lovely indents that ran from his hips toward a cock that was already standing at attention awaiting her ministrations. He may have angry scars from his injuries, but Cam had nothing to be ashamed of. It made her heart sing that he no longer seemed embarrassed for her to see his wounds or his amputation.

Like a butler, he bent at the waist, hand on the shower stall for balance, and swept his arm forward. "After you, Madame."

He positioned the chair in the stall and turned to face her. The chair made the space tight but all the better to get up close and personal. The warm water sluiced down her back creating rivers of pleasure, but nothing compared to the man in front of her and what his mouth was doing to her breasts, her neck, her lips. Her body thrummed. Her pulse pounded in her ears.

Soaping his hands, Cam smoothed them down her back and over her buttocks, pulling her securely against his erection. The steam absorbed the sweet, tropical scent of her shower gel and permeated the air. It was like being lost on their own private island. She marveled at how well he managed on one leg, strong and steady, while leaving her feeling as soft and pliable as warm butter. Cam must have a core of steel to be able to maintain his balance.

His lips moved hungrily down the column of her throat and returned to her breasts. Erotic and thorough, his mouth silently lavished praise. Molten lava pooled in her midsection bubbling and popping and energizing. They'd had fantastic sex several times last night. How could she want him so desperately again? He consumed her. She was quickly reaching the point where she couldn't imagine her life without him.

Her hands slipped up and down his hips, the arousing sensation of slick skin beneath her palms turning her knees to jelly. One hand moved to circle his hard shaft while the fingers of her other hand dug into his tight ass. He groaned and shuddered when she traced the sensitive area below his tip.

"Crystal." Her name sounded like a prayer on his lips as he lowered himself onto the stool. After he sheathed himself in a condom, he tugged on her hands to bring her to him.

Straddling him, she eased onto his length, throwing back her head and moaning as he filled her. A perfect fit. He touched off sparks that no other man had. Her orgasm hit her like a wave lifting her to its crest as she pulsed around him. He growled his release as they exploded before lightly slipping along the foaming water to the shore, their hearts beating in unison.

The shower cooled, and he leaned forward to turn it off. Kissing her deeply, their tongues tangoed until they were both breathless, his arms tightened around her as though he was afraid she might get away.

Looping her arms across his shoulders, she pressed her lips lightly on his neck and sighed. "Mmm, Heaven." The dusting of hair on his chest tickled her breasts as she breathed. "Keep this up and you'll never be able to get rid of me."

"That's a burden I'll just have to live with." She felt his smile curl against her cheek. One of the dogs whined outside the shower stall. "But I suppose we better get moving before we have a riot on our hands."

He pushed the shower door open. She jumped when a cool, wet nose touched her leg. When she wiggled off his lap, Cam growled, and his eyes darkened. Giggling she said, "Haven't you had enough?"

"Never." His hands cupped her breasts, but she backed out of the shower and grabbed her robe.

Leaning over, she wrapped a towel around her hair. "Why don't you take the dogs for a walk and I'll get breakfast?"

He sighed but nodded. "Would you hand me a towel and my crutches?"

Following him into the bedroom, she watched with interest as he carefully dried his stump and attached his prosthesis. He'd been through so much. Abandoned by his father, raised by a single mom—a lovely woman who did the best she could, but they never had much—taking on responsibility at an early age to help out, postponing his dream of college to go into the Army, and then losing his leg. To come back from all of that and to have become this amazing man... took a strength she could barely fathom. She doubted she would have had the courage to do the same.

Glancing at her, he winked and grinned as he laced his sneakers. "Times a wasting, woman. I'm going to expect breakfast when I get back." He stood, kissed her quickly, and left the room, the dogs at his heels. His voice floated back from the front door. "Don't forget to lock up after me."

Ah, yes. That.

She hated reality.

·♥·♥·♥·♥·♥·

CAM STOOPED TO PICK up the box on the front porch and glanced at the sender's address. A local intimate apparel shop. That looked promising, but he'd ask her if she'd ordered it before allowing her to open it. Unlocking the front door, he hummed a tune under his breath. The minute he walked into the house, the tune died on his lips. Crystal stood in the middle of the living room holding her phone in a shaking hand, a stricken look on her face.

Tossing the box on the sofa, he went to her, his heart in his throat, and gathered her in his arms. "Jonathan?"

She buried her face in his chest and he felt her nod. Prying the phone from her fingers, he read the messages, heat burning its way from his stomach to his hairline. This guy was a wacko. He swung from declarations of love to fantasies of their life together to calling her vile things for being with Cam. And the images... a house with a picket fence, another of them at the wedding, and one with blood dripping from a knife with the word 'Cam' superimposed. He'd love it if Jonathan tried to come after him. Most chilling was a series of photos of them at her parent's ranch yesterday. He'd obviously found some way onto the ranch. They'd have to patrol the ridge above the house until Jonathan was stopped.

Holding her at arm's length, he looked into her eyes. The worry, tinged with fear, chewed a hole through his gut. He led her to the sofa and gently pushed her to sit. "I'll get you a glass of water." Scooter, the Beagle, stood on his hind legs and rested his paws on her leg. Her smile as she smoothed the dog's ears eased Cam's anxiety.

When he returned, he stopped dead in his tracks, almost spilling the water. She was holding up a bright red, fur-trimmed sheer negligee that looked like it belonged on a hooker with an expression of utter confusion on her face. The box he'd brought in sat beside her. "*Did you buy this for me?*"

"No, the box was on the front porch. I meant to ask if you'd ordered something before you opened it." He grabbed the garment, stuffed it back in the box, and handed her the water. "Drink." Picking up the box, he carefully riffled through the tissue paper and found a card. '*Can't wait to see you in this. 'J'.*

"Jonathan?" she asked.

Cam nodded. He laid everything out on the sofa and snapped a picture that he emailed to the police. Closing his eyes, an anger coursed through him like he'd never felt before. Not even at the *hajjis* who'd murdered his buddies in combat. "Grab your school supplies and let's get out of here. We'll deal with this later."

# Chapter Ten

♥

A HALF HOUR LATER, Cam perched on a first grader's chair—one of four surrounding a small table. His butt hung over each side and his knees angled toward his chest. He hoped he didn't topple onto the floor. Greedily he unwrapped his breakfast burrito. Biting into the tortilla he had to smother a moan as the aroma of eggs, beans, and green chilies assaulted his nose and made friends with his taste buds.

He looked up and caught Crystal grinning at him. "What? Do I have cheese stuck in my beard?"

Chuckling she brushed her fingertips across his forehead as though brushing away stray locks of hair. Since his military cut didn't allow for that possibility, she must have just wanted to touch him. He liked that idea.

"You remind me of that movie, *Kindergarten Cop*. A bit out of your element but destined to restore order to a chaotic world."

"Little kids scare me shitless." He shook his head and grinned. "I think you'd be the one rescuing me."

"Charging into battle guns blazing, you can handle... but a bunch of six-year-olds makes you want to cower in the corner? You're too funny."

"In battle, I know what I'm doing, and the only one I can mess up... other than the enemy... is me. Being responsible for molding young lives..." Cam shuddered. "I'd be walking on eggshells afraid I'd do or say something to warp them forever." He bit into his second burrito with a vengeance.

"Are you saying you don't want to have children?" Her busy fingers turned a paper napkin into confetti.

"No, I do want kids someday." He swallowed hard to get the bite of food past the lump in his throat. This wasn't a conversation he'd expected to have. "I'm just saying it's not like I had a role model, so being a good dad is uncharted territory for me."

She swept the bits of paper into her palm. "Actually, your experience has given you perfect insight into what it takes to be a wonderful dad. Think back to all the things you wished your dad had done with you, and then be that person." She tossed the paper into the takeout bag and wiped her hands on another napkin. "The biggest part of being a good parent is being there and making sure your children know you love them no matter what. Mistakes...?" She shrugged. "Every parent makes them, and most kids turn out fine."

"Thanks for the pep talk, coach." He could certainly see Crystal as the mother of his children. With her at his side, he couldn't screw them up too badly. Envisioning her belly round with his baby set him back on his heels. Slow down cowboy. Using the table for leverage, he stood. "So, what's next?" His voice coiled like a rattlesnake.

Her expression unreadable, she walked to her collapsible utility cart filled with decorating supplies and pulled out a flat box. Handing it to him she said, "I want these alphabet cards to go over the top of the whiteboard." She laid a picture on the teacher's desk. "See, like this. The train engine angles around this end and the caboose around the other end. Step stool's over there. Push pins are here." She pivoted, her hands on her hips. "I'm going to turn that corner into my reading area." She pointed and wheeled the cart that direction.

Cam picked up the small toolbox he'd brought and set it on the desk. After tacking the train engine and caboose cards where Crystal had indicated, he pulled out his tape measure and marked down the total available space as well as the width of the alphabet cards. He was engrossed in computing the exact placement when Crystal's arms snaked around his waist and her cheek nestled between his shoulder blades. He felt her chuckle against his back.

"I should have known the eyeball approach wouldn't work for you."

He tugged on her arm until she stood beside him. "Measuring saves time." He scrutinized the half-finished reading corner and lifted an eyebrow. "Break time?"

"The bookcases are heavier than I thought. I can't move them into position by myself."

"I'll be right with you."

She hefted the step stool. "If you don't need this, I'd like to use it."

"No, go ahead." He completed his calculations and laid out the cards, resting them on the lip of the whiteboard. As soon as he turned, he grinned. She was hanging a colorful book poster and stretching to push a pin into the top corner. In side profile, her shorts pulled taut and outlined her butt, leaving little to the imagination. Her breasts strained against the soft cotton fabric of her top. Quite a sight. He shook his head like a dog shedding water. Wrong time. Wrong place.

Crystal smiled as he approached. "Does this look straight?"

Cocking his head, he considered her handiwork. "Yeah, I guess so."

Splaying her hands, her face creased in frustration. "Honestly? That's your answer?"

"I'd have to get my level out to be sure, but it looks fine."

Stepping off the stool, she rolled her eyes. "Science guys."

"What do you need me to do?"

"I want the small bookcase moved here." She faced the wall with her hands about shoulder width apart to indicate the spot.

He pursed his lips to keep from smiling. "Might have been easier to move without all the books in it." A playfulness he hadn't felt in years sprang to life. She crossed her arms over her chest and narrowed her eyes. He ducked his head and bit back a grin. Time to keep his mouth shut and get the job done.

After shoving the bookcase into position, he hurried over to help her hang a long chart with each student's name neatly printed followed by a row of blank squares. He assumed the squares would be filled with stickers for completing tasks. "What happens to kids who don't do their reading? Do their squares stay blank?" He'd been that kid and knew the humiliation. He'd had to help his working mom get basic chores done—like laundry, meals, housework. Time for outside reading assignments took second place. It was all he could do to keep up with the math and science homework. Facing a row of blank squares still filled him with dread.

"No, I'd never do that to a child." She brushed her lips against his cheek. "Students will have lots of opportunities to put stickers in those boxes. They can answer questions when I read to them, they can read a page out loud to the class, they can act out a scene from the story, or they can bring in a book to share… Children should feel included."

He pressed his fingers to his lips. Had she known what he'd gone through back then? Always observant, so probably, yes. He edged over to the area rug she'd placed on the floor. "Did you bring any carpet tape? Wouldn't want the kids tripping."

Her gaze swung to the area rug. "Oh my gosh, I hadn't thought about that." She smacked her forehead with the heel of her hand. "Another thing to add to my list."

Cam chuckled. Coming to her rescue was an empowering gig. "Don't worry. I have some in my tool kit."

Once he'd settled himself on the floor, she said, "You and my dad had a nice, long chat. Talk about anything in particular?"

He waited for the sting of pain to hit behind his eyes. It didn't come. Hmmm. Was he ready to talk about what he'd been feeling since his injury? He rubbed his jaw. Best to start slow. "He showed me all the improvements he's made. Good to see him excited again."

"It is." She'd been filling a large, straw basket with percussion and other small musical instruments and paused, her hand poised over the opening. "He talked to me about *that night* and how it wasn't my fault. Got me to thinking, we lay a lot of stuff on ourselves that we don't need to. I feel like I'm finally beginning to let go of the guilt I've been lugging around." She stood and pulled some hats and capes out of her cart, setting them neatly on the top of the bookcase.

"I'm glad." Cam chewed on the inside of his cheek. "Your dad was on a roll yesterday. Told me to avoid the mistakes he made when he was hurt. Focus on what I can do instead of what I can't." He looked away. "Turns out the first list is a lot longer than the second. Wise man."

"Yes, he is." She looked around the room. "I know Dad's accident made me risk-averse, and though I know it wasn't my fault, I'm still not ready to take big chances. Too much can go wrong in life."

Finished applying the carpet tape, Cam got to his feet feeling restless and unsettled. Would she consider him a chance worth taking? Part of him wanted to ask. Part of him feared the answer. Making love to her had changed everything. He wanted more but wasn't convinced that would be in her best interest. "What's left to do?"

"You need to finish putting up the alphabet cards, and I'm going to set up the math center and calendar." She pulled several wide, colorful poster board arrows with writing on them out of the cart. "You can tack these to the wall when you're done." She shuffled through them, reading the titles and pointing to specific areas as she did. "Reading. Math. Art. Science. Cubbies. I'd like them at an angle." She held one of the arrows up to demonstrate before setting them on a nearby table.

"On it, boss." He stopped short of clicking his heels and saluting. She might not see the humor.

"Tomorrow I'll set up the cubbies, art center, science area, and put away the textbooks and supplies the school district provides. Today, I want to make sure we get out of here in plenty of time for you to make your orientation."

He didn't like the idea of leaving her alone, but she'd have the dogs, and he'd monitor the house remotely. He had the police station on speed dial. It wouldn't be long before he started work and she was teaching. He had to trust he'd taught her enough about self-defense and situational awareness to stay safe when he couldn't be with her. His protective instincts churned in his gut, but he had to live with the fact that he couldn't wrap her in bubble wrap.

# Chapter Eleven

♥

CRYSTAL GAZED OUT THE driver-side window at the passing scenery. Not that the view was much different there than from the passenger window, but it gave her a chance to drink in the profile of the man behind the wheel. No matter how many times she studied Cam, she always saw something new—several tiny scars along his jaw, a scattering of random dark freckles along his cheekbones, creases on his forehead from his intense expression.

He turned his head and smiled. She wanted to run her fingertips over the laugh lines that radiated out from the corners of his eyes. "Thank you," she said.

"For what?"

"For a wonderful week." Cam brought her hand to his lips and her heart fluttered.

"You're welcome. What was your favorite thing?"

"The Thai cooking class... was unexpected and fun. I had no idea you were so handy in the kitchen. I've never kayaked on Lady Bird Lake before. I'll admit I was a bit anxious about paddling out on the water in that tippy thing but I'm glad you talked me in to it." Reclining in her seat, she folded her hands in her lap, sighed deeply, and everything in her calmed. "My favorite thing though," —the familiar flutter tickled her belly— "was spending time with you." She turned her head against the seat and smiled at him. Not to mention those long nights of lovemaking. "It also helped that Jonathan went radio silent."

"Now that the cops have tracked him down for the second time and put the fear of God in him—along with all the business he's losing—maybe he's decided it's time to relocate."

The doubt in Cam's expression matched the doubt constricting her breath, but she put on a happy face. "New topic. I'm thrilled your new company supports employees who want to finish their education."

A grin spread across his face. "Yeah, that was a perk I hadn't expected. Time off with pay to take classes." He did a quick drum beat on the steering wheel and nodded his head in time to the music. "I forgot to tell you, I talked to a counselor yesterday afternoon. Put together a degree plan and registered for two classes this Fall. Should take about two years to get my BS. What the G.I. Bill doesn't cover, the company will. It's one sweet deal."

He looked so proud she wanted to lean across the console and hug him. She'd save that for later when they sneaked off for some alone time after her dad's birthday party wound down.

Later that afternoon, as the clock approached four, Crystal was ready to escape. From the time people started arriving at eleven till now, they had feasted on barbeque, danced to country music—Cam had some impressive moves—caught up on gossip, and heaped well-wishes upon her dad. Some peace and quiet with Cam sounded like heaven.

Now that only a few diehards remained, Cam and Crystal took their leave, promising to return in time to help clean up. Throughout the day they'd endured speculative glances, whispered conversations that stopped when they approached, knowing smiles—and their two mothers' heads together, probably planning their wedding. Married to Cam. That fantasy put a smile on her face as wide as the Rio Grande River. If that was the eventual outcome, she'd be the happiest woman in the world.

·♥·♥·♥·♥·♥·

FROM HIS NEW VANTAGE point on the ridge opposite of where he'd been before, Jonathan watched them drive off in the little Gator they'd used last weekend. He'd known that sending the photos of them on the ranch would make them extra vigilant, but he couldn't resist. Ranch hands patrolled the area, but he'd been able to evade them. Today, he was also prepared to follow them. The dogs were with them again. That meant he couldn't get too close or the mutts might pick up his scent. He'd also seen Cam tuck a rifle under the seat and had no doubt the man knew how to use it.

How could she take off with this guy? A nothing when she could have Jonathan. He straddled his mountain bike, gripping the handlebars so tightly blood stopped flowing to his fingers. Securing his helmet, he set off in the general direction the pair had gone. This time of year, he should be able to follow the dust trail and still maintain his distance. On his bike, he could keep a low profile and make good use of the rock outcroppings, scrub brush, and hollows.

They stopped on a knoll and made their way down to a small grassy area along the river. Over the centuries the water had carved out a concave wall in the limestone that towered over the area. Water trickled over the edge and into the river below. The change in elevation and the numerous trees gave Jonathan a perfect vantage point to observe from above without being detected.

Cam spread out a blanket. Crystal set a small cooler beside it. The dogs circled the area, exploring with their noses to the ground before settling in the shade of a tree. Cam and Crystal quickly shed their clothes. God. Crystal was as beautiful as he'd imagined. Should have been his hands on those luscious curves. Crystal stepped into the water and waded out until she could sink to her neck. Cam sat on a rock and removed his artificial leg. Disgusting. With the aid of a crutch, he stood and dove into the deep water where Crystal floated, her belly and breasts glistening in the sun. Jonathan set the camera on a short tripod and snapped a few photos.

The couple embraced and kissed, laughing and joyous. Their bodies fused together. Cam put his mouth on her breast and she threw her head back. Jonathan ground his teeth and started forward. All three dogs' heads swiveled and their ears twitched. With no recourse, he flattened himself against a tree, hardly daring to breath. When the dog's heads again rested on their paws, he lowered himself to the ground and lay prone. Reaching inside his pack, he retrieved his binoculars. His arms shook as he watched their foreplay. The taste of dust was chalky in his mouth.

Before long, they emerged from the water, Crystal supporting Cam as he hopped to the blanket. How could she degrade herself like this? Jonathan switched his camera to record, to capture their lovemaking. Fantasizing it was he and not Cam she touched, he hardened, rolled to his side, and pushed his spandex biker pants down his hips. Closing his eyes, he could feel Crystal beneath him, her fingers digging into *his* back instead of Cam's. Her moans of pleasure drifted to him on the gentle breeze, and they were for him. His heart pounded in his ears.

He squinted at the camera's display screen. They had switched position and Crystal was on top, riding him, her breasts captured in Cam's hands. Her chin lowered to her chest as her body tightened in what must be her release. Jonathan pressed his lips together, stifling his groan as his seed spilled onto the ground.

Crystal collapsed onto Cam. His hands smoothed up and down her back. Possessive and intimate, probably whispering lewd things in her ear. Eventually they lay on their sides facing each other—talking quietly, smiling, and touching. Cam rose on his elbow, reached across Crystal's naked form, and pulled two bottles from the cooler. After opening them, he handed one to Crystal. The tableau playing out in front of Jonathan continued for another hour until Crystal got up and reclaimed the prosthetic and crutch Cam had left on the boulder by the river.

By the time she'd returned, he'd put on his boxers and dangled her bra and panties from one finger. She knelt beside him and they kissed again before she bent down and kissed Cam's stump. How could she let that half-man touch her? He must have some power over her. That was the only explanation. Jonathan had to rescue her. Set her free from whatever spell Cam had cast over her. Mine. Mine. Mine... rattled in his brain like a hard rain against a window.

# Chapter Twelve

♥

A FEW DAYS LATER, Crystal was placing her lunch dishes in the dishwasher when her phone chimed. Cam was helping his mom pack for the move to her new house, and she'd been expecting a status update. She would have gone with him, but she needed to finalize her lesson plans for next week. Besides, he needed some alone time with his mom.

She smiled that sappy kind of smile one does when hearing from the person she loves. Loves. The word sat on her tongue like buttercream icing. They hadn't been together long as a couple, but she knew she wanted to spend the rest of her life with him.

Opening the message, her brows creased in confusion. '*Meet me at our spot by the river at 3:00. Leave the dogs. I'll be waiting. Cam.*'

Cam's number, but his message was odd. He usually insisted that if she was alone, she have the dogs with her. Maybe because they hadn't heard from Jonathan in a while, and he'd closed up his insurance office, Cam believed they didn't need to be as cautious. Shrugging she tapped out a reply. '*See you soon. Crystal.*'

Humming under her breath, she pulled the picnic basket out of the pantry. Adding crackers, cheese, fresh pears, and a nice bottle of Pinot Noir to the plates, glasses, and silverware already in the basket, she closed its lid. A blanket and towels waited in the trunk of her car.

After refilling the dog's water dish and scooping dry food into their bowls, she picked up the basket and left. Pulling out her phone, she sent a text. '*I'm on my way.*'

On the drive to her parent's ranch, excitement beat a happy tune in her chest. Was Cam planning to propose? She'd caught him staring at her with a thoughtful expression more than once in the past few days. Since they'd been intimate, he'd opened up, but was still holding a part of himself back. She'd known he thought growing up poor meant he couldn't make her happy, that she deserved better. She could only hope he'd finally gotten past that misconception. All she wanted from a man was someone who loved her as much as she loved him. The rest they'd work out.

When she pulled into her parent's yard, no one was about. Not surprising. Dad and the ranch hands must be out checking on the cattle and her mom was most likely at the high school getting ready for the new term. Plucking the keys to the Gator off the hook in the equipment shed, she transferred the picnic supplies, left a note for her dad, and slipped behind the wheel.

Parking on the level spot by the trail leading down to the river, she looked around. Not spying any other vehicles, she shrugged—must have arrived before Cam. No matter. She'd set out their snack and wait. It would be nice to have a few minutes to relax and let her mind drift.

As she started down the path, she noticed a mountain bike propped against a tree. She didn't know Cam had a bike. Then again, she hadn't spent enough time at his place yet to know everything he had. But where was his truck? She hadn't seen it at her parents. Her steps slowed, and unease made the hair on her neck bristle. Surely he wouldn't have ridden his bike the ten miles from his mom's house in town to here. Something didn't add up.

"Cam?" She cocked her head side-to-side trying to pick up any sound. A twig snapped, and her feet automatically moved to retreat up the trail.

Jonathan stepped out from behind a tree. She gasped, nearly dropping the picnic basket and blanket. Before she could move, he closed the distance between them and latched on to her arm.

"Glad you could make it." His voice—pressure cooker taut plus the wild look in his eyes—chilled her to the bone.

"What are you doing here?" she croaked past her suddenly dry mouth. His grip tightened as she attempted to break his hold.

"Isn't it obvious?" His forehead furrowed as though he really didn't understand her confusion. "We belong to each other."

The blood drained from her face and her hands grew clammy. What could she say to placate him? Everything in her screamed run... hide.

"Of course we do. I've been so foolish. Look, I brought us a picnic." She wiggled the basket in her hand. "Would you like me to set it out?" If she hit him with the basket, could she hurt him enough to get away? Probably not.

He squeezed her arm harder and she winced. "Liar. You came here expecting to meet *him*." Spittle hit her cheek. "*Whore*." He shook her arm. "*You prefer that half man over me*?" His voice rose harsh like a winter wind and she recoiled.

Jonathan vibrated with rage. She had to calm him down. Think. She wasn't that scared kid anymore. Use what Cam had taught her about self-defense. First, she needed to get this stuff out of her arms so she could actually do something if the opportunity presented itself.

"Maybe I didn't think I had a chance with you." She kept her voice meek and opened her eyes wide to look sincere. To convince him that what was true, wasn't. "You're too good for me." Letting her shoulders slump she looked down at the ground, hoping she looked meek as a puppy caught doing something it shouldn't.

He shook her arm again, but his grip loosened. "You've had sex with him. Here. A few days ago. How can I trust what you say?" His handsome face flushed with anger.

*Good God. He'd been here? He'd seen them?* Her stomach curdled like bad milk and she thought she might throw up. "I'm sorry to have disappointed you. I must have been under a spell, but now you've rescued me. Thank you."

"I'll always be here for you. How could you betray me like that?" He snatched the blanket off her arm and hurled it aside. Wrenching the picnic basket from her hands, he flung it away. She flinched at the sound of breaking glass as the basket tumbled over the rocks and into the water.

Before she had a chance to react, he enveloped her in a bear hug. Cam's self-defense training took over. The top of her head pushed against his shoulder at the same time she stuck her butt out and shoved her hands into his lower abdomen to create enough space for her knee to connect with his groin. When he doubled over, her foot struck his knee with as much force as she could muster. Heart racing and blood rushing in her ears, she spun away and made a mad dash for the trail. Not fast enough. Her entire body sagged as pain exploded in her head.

·♥·♥·♥·♥·♥·

PAPER RUSTLED AS CAM wrapped the last of the knick-knacks from his mom's curio cabinet. He had no idea why this collection of miscellaneous ceramic salt and pepper shakers fascinated her, but they did, and he was fine with that. The scent of popcorn filled the air as his mom bustled into the room.

Dark eyes sparkled against her olive skin. Her once jet-black hair was now streaked with gray but styled in a chin-length bob that made her look ten years younger than the sixty-five she was. Petite, the top of her head barely reaching his chin, her curves more rounded now than in his youth, she still managed to cut a striking figure. And her energy... she put him to shame.

"*Querido,*" she eased gracefully into one of the dining room chairs, "I thought we needed a little snack." She handed him one of the bowls she'd carried in. "You've worked so hard today, and we haven't had a chance to talk."

Accepting the bowl, he sat down beside her and refrained from rolling his eyes. He knew exactly what she wanted to talk about. Was there a mother—ever—who didn't want to meddle in her son's love life? He bit back a grin. Nosey, but he owed her so much.

"Thanks Mom. Looks like there's not much left to pack except the kitchen stuff." He leaned over and gave her a quick hug. "Ten days, Mom, and you'll move into your own home." He swallowed past the lump in his throat at the tears glistening in her eyes. It felt good to be able to do this for her. He popped one of the warm kernels into his mouth. "Extra butter. Just the way I like it."

Patting his knee, she said, "Of course. A mother never forgets what her child likes." She glanced around the room a hint of nostalgia in her expression. "I've been here a long time. Lots of memories." She smiled at him. "You were just a baby when we moved here but I'm ready for a new start." Arching her brow, she asked, "What about you? Are you ready?"

No sense pretending he didn't understand her reference. "Yeah, I am." He set his empty bowl on the table. "It was hard leaving the service. I'd thought that was my purpose, my life." He shrugged but the achy emptiness he'd once felt wasn't there. "I miss my buddies but I've got the skills to do other things. Things I hope I like just as much as being a soldier."

His mom's smile was about as subtle as a guy sliding into home base. "Could Crystal have anything to do with finding a new purpose?"

He couldn't stop the ping in his chest or the loopy grin on his face. "Maybe. I like her, Mom."

"I like her too, son. Always have. Have you said anything to her yet?"

He saw her assessing look and sighed. "No. We haven't been dating long, and I wanted to get my life situated first."

She did that head shake that mothers do when they think their child is denser than a rock. "Because you think you're not good enough for her? Just because you didn't have the things she had growing up? Because you were poor?"

Everything inside him stilled.

"Sweetheart, you do realize that none of that matters to Crystal. You're an honorable man. A strong man. That's what matters to her." She squeezed his arm and stood. "Don't let the words go unsaid too long or some other man will scoop her up."

She looked down at him. "Since you're still staying with Crystal, I assume the Jonathan situation hasn't resolved itself." She gathered the empty bowls. "We've all switched insurance agents and said good riddance."

"We haven't heard from him in over a week so we're hoping he's moved on." Cam rubbed the back of his neck. "It makes me nervous though that he's just dropped off the radar. It's too neat." He stood and was moving the chairs back into place when his phone rang.

"Hey Fiona," he said. "What's up?" His mom paused on her way to the kitchen. "What do you mean she's not at home?" He listened and with each tick of the second hand, he felt like he was being pulled under water and couldn't get back to the surface. "She hasn't answered her phone?" His lungs were about to burst. "I'll check her phone and see what I can find out. It's odd that she left without the dogs." It took a herculean effort to keep the panic out of his voice as he disconnected.

"Is something wrong?" his mom asked.

"Fiona stopped by to have coffee with Crystal and she's not there. She'd said she'd be home all afternoon." With shaking fingers, he opened the app on his phone that gave him access to Crystal's phone.

"Maybe she just ran out to the store?" He could feel his mom peering around his arm and watching him check Crystal's phone. "You can see her calls?"

"Yeah Mom, I can." His mind ticked off each fact. Nothing on her call log except one incoming from Fiona. His heart stopped when he saw the spoofed text messages. Cam's number showed as the sending number. Crystal obviously hadn't suspected that it came from someone else. She had no idea how easy it was to spoof another person's phone number. With a few keystrokes he forwarded the string of messages to Josh, so he could coordinate with the police. The texts were about an hour old. If he hurried, he might catch her before she left her parent's house for the fake rendezvous.

"Mom, I gotta go. Call Jessalyn and Harry and tell them I'm on my way. I'll be there in ten minutes. Tell them I'll explain everything when I get there but Jonathan may have Crystal."

# Chapter Thirteen

♥

Gravel spewed as Cam barreled into the yard at the Kincaid ranch. He screeched to a halt and jumped out on a run. Swiftly he strode to where Harry, Jessalyn, Zach, Nate, and Wayne waited.

"Josh called right after your mom did and filled us in. Crystal's car is here and one of the Gators is missing. I'm guessing Crystal has it," Harry said. "Where do you think Jonathan is holding her?"

The pinched looks on everyone's faces pushed Cam's already soaring heartrate into something he wasn't sure was sustainable. "I'm guessing the old swimming hole we used as kids. Not sure how Jonathan found out about it, but that seems the most likely spot from his message to her."

"What do you want us to do?" Zach asked.

Cam slipped into his military mission mode. "I'm going to check out the swimming hole Crystal and I visited recently." His fists clenched at the memories of what they'd shared there, and a red-hot burn built in his gut. "Zach and Nate, remember that quarry closer to your property where we used to swim sometimes?"

They nodded.

"You check there, just in case I'm wrong."

"Dad's organizing our ranch hands to help with a search. They'll be here soon," Nate added.

"Great. The more the better." His gaze shifted to Harry and Wayne. "I'll take my truck, and you two follow me in the other Gator. I know you won't be able to keep up, but you know where I'm talking about."

More nods.

"Don't worry about falling behind. I'm fine on my own. I'll leave my truck about a mile from the swimming hole and jog the rest of the way, so he won't hear me coming. By the time you get there I'll have assessed the situation and how to handle it."

A few of the ranch hands joined them. Cam angled his head toward the ranch foreman. "Why don't you guys split up and check the remote line shacks, cattle shelters, or anyplace else he might hide?" He glanced up at the clip clop of horses' hooves.

"I had a bunch of horses saddled in case we needed them," the ranch foreman explained.

"Good thinking," Cam said. "Is everyone armed?" All nodded. "Okay, check your weapons and ammo, and silence your phones. We'll communicate by text message from here on. Let's move out." The men did as asked, and vaulted into the saddles.

"Cam, what should I do?" Jessalyn asked.

"Wait here and when the others arrive, let them know what's going on and where we're at."

Cam strode to his truck, unlocked his gun safe, and removed his sniper rifle and sidearm. He'd been an Electronic Warfare Specialist, not a sniper, but he'd qualified and was still a damn good shot. With an efficiency born of military training, he checked his rifle and Glock and swung into his truck.

It struck him as he raced out of the yard, no one had questioned his ability to do what he'd outlined. They all accepted that he'd be able to jog that last mile over rough terrain, sneak up on Jonathan, and protect Crystal. He wished he had their faith. Shoving the fear and uncertainty deep into his gut he jerked to a stop about a mile from his destination.

He'd been running and working out every day since he left Walter Reed and had built up to five miles a day. Physically he was probably ready… but untested. Guess he was going to find out. Fear couldn't take over. He had to push images of Crystal in Jonathan's hands into the depths of his soul and focus. Slinging the rifle strap over his shoulder and tucking the Glock into the holster at his waist, he set off at a brisk pace. The rifle bounced against his back, bringing back memories of battlefield action. Nearing the bluff that overlooked the river, he dropped to the ground and belly-crawled to the edge.

Jonathan had Crystal by the arm, shaking her. Cam watched, his jaw clenching, as Crystal's head snapped back. Filling his lungs and slowing his heartrate, he steadied his rifle. No shot. Crystal was in the way. He could wait for a shot to open up. From what he could see of Jonathan through his scope, he might murder Crystal at any moment. He couldn't risk waiting. Fear ripped through him and a cold sweat trickled down his back. Sucking in a deep breath, he closed his eyes and willed the calculating part of his brain to take over. He had to be the man Crystal needed.

Inching down the path to the river, Cam placed his feet carefully. Any movement of the earth would alert

Jonathan, and Cam would lose the element of surprise. As he reached the bottom, Jonathan flung the picnic basket into the river and grabbed Crystal in a bear hug. Before Cam's feet could move, Crystal put her self-defense training to good use. She kneed Jonathan in the groin and broke away, then darted toward the path Cam was on.

He stepped into the clearing just as Jonathan produced a billy club that he brought down on Crystal's head. He saw recognition in her eyes as she pitched forward. She knew he was here. Cam caught her and eased her to the ground, angling his body so the next blow landed on his shoulder. With adrenaline masking the pain, Cam braced on his arms and swung his right leg in an arc. He caught Jonathan on the knee, and the man staggered back, howling in rage.

Cam jumped to his feet, amazed at how well his prosthesis responded. When Jonathan charged, Cam deflected his punch and swiveled, kicking the other man's feet out from beneath him. Jonathan hit the ground but rolled away before Cam could pin him down. Scrambling to his feet, Jonathan pulled a knife, and the two men circled.

Crystal moaned. She was alive, but Cam couldn't let anything, even Crystal, pull his focus until Jonathan was neutralized. Jonathan jabbed the knife at Cam from a safe distance, circling him like a bear. Cam closed the distance between them, blocked the knife thrust, twisted Jonathan's arm, and the knife went flying. Hands fisted, Cam punched Jonathan in the throat and the man staggered back, lost his balance, and tumbled over the boulder and into the rocks below. He lay still, at an awkward angle.

Shouts, followed by footsteps sliding down the path, told Cam reinforcements had arrived. While his entire being wanted to rush to Crystal, his first duty was to make sure Jonathan couldn't cause any more harm. "Someone check on Crystal," Cam shouted. "Jonathan fell onto the rocks, and I'm going to secure him."

Sliding down the boulder until his feet touched the pebbled ground, he drew his sidearm and slowly approached the prone man. Jonathan still hadn't moved. Cam put his knee on the man's back and checked his pulse.

Zach appeared at the top of the boulder. "Anything?" he asked.

"He's gone." Cam shook his head and checked Jonathan for weapons just in case he'd missed a pulse. He found a handgun and laid it out of reach. "How's Crystal?" He could hardly get the words out. His mouth felt like the Sahara.

"Nate and Wayne are giving her first aid. She's breathing and groggy and needs to be seen by a doctor. That bump on her head may need stitches, and it looks like she dislocated her shoulder. Harry called the police as soon as we caught up with you. They should be here soon."

Relief nearly leveled Cam. "Thank God she's okay."

"By the way, you're bleeding."

He glanced at his arm. "Must have been nicked by the knife. Nothing serious." Standing, he dusted his hands on his pants. "How'd you and Nate get here so fast? Weren't you heading to the other side of the ranch?"

"Dad and his posse pulled in just after you left. We sent them out there and decided to join Wayne and Harry in case you needed reinforcements." Zach lifted his hat, his expression grim. "We got here in time to see you fighting and Jonathan go over the edge. It was an accident. You've got witnesses."

"You saw me pull this gun out of Jonathan's waistband?" Cam asked pointing to the revolver.

"Yup."

"I'm going to leave him here but I'll bring the gun up with me." The adrenalin rush receded like a wave pulling away from the shore. The shakes rippled through him. His arm shrieked. This was the point in the old WWII movie where the soldier stuck a cigarette in his mouth with trembling fingers and inhaled the calm. Cam didn't smoke but would have appreciated the calm.

After making his way back to the grassy area above the river, Cam rushed to Crystal's side. Her ashen face, the blood-soaked bandage at the back of her head, and her arm strapped to her body shook Cam to his core. If Jonathan wasn't already dead, Cam would have finished the job. Slumping beside her, he cupped her face in his hands his thumbs smoothing back her hair. As much as he wanted to gather her in his arms, he knew better than to move her. Her eyes fluttered open. The adoration he saw humbled him. He may not deserve it, deserve her, but he was hooked. He'd stay with her as long as she would have him.

Her hand stroked his cheek. Her touch, the warmth returning to her skin, the new color in her cheeks, her steady breathing reassured him. She would survive. He released the breath that had caught in his chest. He'd hear her laughter again. See the kindness and joy in her eyes. Taste those luscious lips. Feel her womanly curves beneath his palms. Smell that rose scent in her hair. He opened his mouth to tell her what she meant to him when her eyes drifted shut. The blood loss and struggle had drained her. She needed to rest. He pressed his lips to her forehead. They'd talk later.

Voices and footsteps sounded from the path. Pebbles bounced down the path and stopped nearby. The paramedics and police had arrived. While the EMTs worked on Crystal, the police pulled the men aside individually and took preliminary statements. Once Crystal was stabilized, one of the EMTs gave Cam a once-over. Other than bandaging a few cuts and where the knife had nicked his arm, they declared him healthy. The coroner arrived, the crime techs did their thing, and Jonathan was eventually zipped into a body bag and hauled away. By the time the EMTs hoisted the gurney with Crystal on it into their waiting ambulance, Cam felt like a piece of ground beef.

A more subdued group trudged back up the path to their vehicles and horses and returned to the ranch. This day served as a reminder that one could only count on the moment in front of them. Nothing else was certain.

# Chapter Fourteen

♥

CRYSTAL FLOATED IN AND out of awareness. Snippets of time made up her reality. Her brother and Nate giving her first aid. Cold. Cam holding her, his face a portrait of torment. Her dad being lifted into the ambulance and riding with her to the hospital holding her hand. Doctors and nurses poking and prodding. Pain exploding in her head and searing through her shoulder like fire. X-rays. Blessed painkillers. Shoulder manipulated back into place. Cam waiting for her when the nurses wheeled her to a hospital room. They planned to keep her overnight for observation.

Cam bent and kissed her, his lips soft and cool on hers. His calloused hand was gentle as he brushed hair away from her forehead. His face was already beginning to discolor from the fight. *Jonathan was dead*. She started.

"You're safe." Cam's voice crooned like a lullaby in her ear. "He can't hurt you anymore." He stroked her hair again. "I've got to go back to the house. The police want to check it to make sure Jonathan didn't leave any booby-traps, and I need to take care of the dogs."

She gripped his arm. "Are the dogs okay? You don't think he could have left a bomb or something?" Heat entered her voice. "I've had it with feeling helpless." Chased by anxiety and fueled by anger, the words tumbled out. His lips brushed hers again. Calm. Reassuring. Solid. "I did it, didn't I? Defended myself?"

"The dogs are fine. The police visit is just a precaution and yes, you did. I never doubted you would." He enveloped her good hand in his. "Your mom is going to spend the night here with you, and I'll be back in the morning to take you home."

Pushing out her bottom lip she asked, "Can't I go home now? Hospitals are not exactly the most restful places." Forget the traumatic memories that hospitals, especially this hospital, held.

"Nobody likes being in the hospital, but we have to make sure nothing else shows up. It's the safe thing to do," Cam said.

She liked the way he kept touching her, as though to reassure himself she wasn't a figment of his imagination. She drew a calming breath and exhaled slowly. "Tomorrow. You promise?"

"Tomorrow," Cam said touching his lips to hers once more, unleashing a burst of pleasure that warmed her all the way through. "I'll call you after the police leave." With that he turned and left, taking a bit of her heart with him.

Once the rest of her family departed and her mom had curled up on the sleeper chair, Crystal turned the day's events over in her head. Tears trickled out of the corners of her eyes. A man was dead. She'd accepted that she hadn't done anything to encourage his behavior, but still, a man was dead and that made her feel hollow inside. When her focus shifted to Cam, light replaced the hollowness. He'd come for her. He'd fought for her. Like a fairytale but real.

That both excited and scared her. He did have a penchant for taking risks. That made her uncomfortable but if she were honest, that's also what attracted her to him. Secretly she'd always wished she could be a bit more like him. Brave and bold. Now that the danger had passed, would he stay with her or would he slip out of her life? Casual friends again, despite what they had shared? Did he feel the same way about her that she did about him? Gradually her eyes shut, and her breathing evened. Other than the times a nurse disturbed her to take her vitals and check her IV drip, Crystal slept deeply.

Cam collected her the next morning. Gently she brushed her fingertips over the dark circles under his eyes. "Rough night?" Understandable, given the punishment his body had taken yesterday.

He nodded and handed her the clothes she'd asked him to bring. "Glad to see you look rested." She chewed on her lip. He hadn't kissed her yet.

"Pain meds will do that for you. Mom signed me out before she left, so as soon as I change, we can leave."

The dogs greeted them at her door, their tails thumping against the floor. If they weren't so well-behaved, they'd have been all over her. Cam had been strangely quiet on the drive home, so it felt good to see some enthusiasm at her return.

Cam wandered into the kitchen and set the pain meds and antibiotics the doctor had sent home with her on the counter. Raising the bag with her bloodied and torn clothing he asked, "What do you want me to do with these?"

She shuddered. "That was one of my favorite outfits, but I never want to see it again. Toss them."

"Figured," he said his expression grim.

As he headed out to the garage, she walked to the refrigerator and removed the pitcher of iced tea. It annoyed her that he found her scowling at a glass tipped on its side and tea dripping over the edge of the counter.

He pursed his lips and did his best to hide his amusement, but the twinkle in his eyes and the movement of his chest gave him away.

She socked him in the arm. "Don't laugh at me." How frustrating to have the simplest of tasks elude her but she had to chuckle along with him. Cam was infectious and exactly what she needed. He held up the mirror she needed to look in to. The one where a confident, strong woman stared back at her.

"Wouldn't think of it." He kissed her neck and picked up a sponge to mop up the mess.

Her heart did a jitterbug. Finally. She'd been afraid he would start pushing her away.

After pouring two glasses, he carried them to the dining room. Pulling out a chair for her, he helped her get settled and then sat down.

"Guess I'm going to have to rethink my routine. Thankfully I didn't damage any tissue or break a bone, so the sling can come off in two weeks, but it will take physical therapy and time to get back to normal." She raised her eyes to the ceiling and shook her head slowly. "With school starting next week, it's going to be interesting." She sucked in a breath and decided the new confident her might as well rip off the Band-Aid. "Are you planning on moving back to your place, or will you stay with me a while?"

"I'll stay long enough to get you back on your feet."

"Then you'll leave?" she asked.

"Do you want me to stay longer?"

113

"Of course. We're friends." Her fingers rested on his arm. "And I thought we were becoming more than friends, much more." She didn't like the tic along his jaw. Fear slithered down her spine.

"Maybe that was a mistake. Maybe we were just caught up in the moment, and it didn't mean anything other than two people clinging together in a crisis." He looked down at her hand and swallowed.

She studied his profile. She wasn't going to take the safe path. It was time to put her feelings out there.

"It wasn't a mistake for me." She placed her good hand flat on the table. "I love you Cam. If you don't feel the same about me, then you'll have to tell me so."

He closed his eyes. When he opened them, he gripped her hand. "It's going to take me years to get my life together. I don't have much to offer, and I don't know if this job is what I really want to do." He placed his fingers under her chin and turned her head. "The last two days have proved to me that I don't have to settle. I can do whatever I want. I was the one setting limits for myself. What if I decide to go back into the Army after I've gotten my degree? Or the police force? Would you still want me?"

Her heart thumped like a jackhammer. He was worried she couldn't accept him for who he is? And why wouldn't he? "Remember when you asked if I could have married a soldier and been happy?"

"Yes, and I also remember your answer." He rubbed the back of his neck. "It's your fault, you know. You see me as the man I want to be, and you've made it possible for me to see myself as that man. I can't turn back now."

He looked so fatalistic. Crystal leaned in and kissed his cheek. "And I wouldn't want you to. Since that talk, I've learned a lot about myself. What I want and what I don't want. I'm tired of hiding. I want to live life to the fullest. Take some risks and know that if I fall, I can bounce back."

"You're saying you'd be okay if I wanted to be more than a desk jockey? You could live with me having a riskier occupation?" He cocked a brow challenge in his expression.

"I'm not saying I wouldn't worry about you. It wouldn't be easy, but I never want to hold you back from doing what you love... whatever that might be. I'm willing to sacrifice a little peace of mind. It'd be worth it to be with you."

A grin spread across his face. "You think so? You really think I can make you happy?"

"I know so. You're everything I want. Kind, honorable, resilient, determined, and you'd move heaven and earth to protect those you care about. Not only do I love you, I respect you. Besides, I'm a rancher's daughter. I'm well acquainted with life's uncertainties. I've learned I can deal with it and fight my way to the top." She tapped the table with her fingernail. "You haven't answered my question yet. Do you love me?"

"With all my heart." He stood and pulled her to her feet. Careful of her injured shoulder, he gathered her in his arms, lowered his head, and kissed her until they were both panting like they'd run a 5K. "I love you. You're a dream come true. One I thought I shouldn't aspire to. You're Texas ranching royalty, and me, I'm a nobody." He held a finger to her lips. "I know that never meant anything to you, but it did to me. Call it pride. I always felt like you deserved more than me." He sighed. "I've come to realize that the true measure of a man isn't his net worth but what he stands for, his values, and how he treats other people. By that measure, I've come to believe I'm worthy."

She felt like she was glowing brighter than the sun and about ready to float away with joy. "Are you saying you're going to stay with me on a permanent basis?"

"On one condition." Holding her hand, he got down on one knee. "Will you marry me, Crystal? Keep reminding me that I am the man you see me as?"

She knelt down with him, so she could stare into his eyes. "Yes. More than anything in this world, I want to be your wife. While I'm not ready to take up sky diving, I want to challenge myself. I want you to challenge me and I want you at my side to catch me if need be."

"I promise you that whatever comes our way, we'll face it together. We'll support each other through life's ups and downs. Our love will keep us strong. I can't imagine a day without you. You make me whole." With that, he stood and sealed their promise with a kiss.

# *Epilogue*

♥

"SHE CERTAINLY IS A busy little thing." Crystal steadied the baby side-stepping from person-to-person. She was sitting in a circle visiting with family and friends at her parent's annual Fourth of July barbeque.

"That she is," said Ashley. "Chasing her around all day sure made it easier to get my figure back."

"I don't know how you do it," Crystal said as chubby hands wrapped around her fingers. The baby used the assist to reach for a plate on the nearby dessert table. "Keeping up with your accounting clients and an active baby... You *are* a glutton for punishment."

"I don't want to lose the client base I've built up. Luckily, one of the perks of being your own boss is that you get to set your own schedule. Zack helps and..." she patted her mother-in-law's knee, "I have a very flexible babysitter." Ashley pushed the plate her daughter had targeted away from the edge.

Proud grandma, Gloria June, beamed. "I finally have a little girl to dress in pink and frills. I was beginning to think this family could only produce boys."

They all laughed as the baby lost her balance and plopped on her thickly-diapered butt. Gloria June scooped her up and blew raspberries on the baby's cheek before tears could fall.

"It won't be long now before she'll have a cousin to play with." Lauren rubbed her extended belly. "Three more weeks, and this guy will join the party." She reached over and squeezed Gloria June's hand. "I know, another boy, but maybe our next one will be a girl."

"Do you think you'll miss stepping away from your family therapy practice for a while?" Fiona asked.

"Like Ashley, I don't want to give up what I've built but I also want some time to bond with my baby." She shrugged. "Life requires tradeoffs to focus on what's really important. I'm leaving my patients in good hands. My partners will make sure their psychological needs are met until I'm ready to return." Lauren glanced over at her husband, Nate, standing around the grill with the other men and smiled. "For now, I'd just be thrilled to see my feet again."

Josh caught Fiona's eye and nudged his brothers. The trio broke away from the group around the grill and ambled over to join their wives. Zach lifted his daughter from his mother's arms and tossed her in the air. The baby squealed in delight and then wriggled to be put down. Nate sat on the ground at Lauren's feet and idly ran his hand up and down her calf. Josh stood behind Fiona and placed his hands on her shoulders.

Fiona gazed up at her husband and smiled shyly. "Josh and I have some news. Come January, Chad will have a brother or sister."

After the rounds of congratulations and back slapping subsided, Ashley turned to Crystal. "So, how's married life treating you?"

"The first month has gone very well. No complaints here." She glanced at her husband, who was deep in conversation with her dad. "Cam is happier than he thought he'd be doing cybersecurity work at JMI but once he's finished his degree at the end of next year, he may look into applying to the police department."

"You'd be okay with that?" Lauren asked.

"Sure. Whatever makes Cam happy makes me happy. There's a part of him that still wants to chase bad guys, and if regular police work is the direction he wants to go, I'll support him. But he also loves the challenge of digging into computers and other devices to help victims get justice, so becoming a digital forensic specialist is still on the table. I'm hoping he takes the forensic path because I'd worry less, but I'm behind him no matter what."

Crystal waved her hand when she spotted Cam's mom walking toward them on the arm of Jay Armstrong, her new significant other. Crystal couldn't remember a time when Mary had someone special in her life. It was good to see her blossom, and she suspected the couple would soon make their relationship permanent.

Yes, Crystal thought, contentment filtered through her light and airy as a cloud. She and the people in her life had carved out their bit of happiness. That didn't mean thunder wouldn't occasionally roll across their landscapes, but family and love would give them the strength and courage to handle the dark times.

Cam strolled up to her, pulled her to her feet, and waltzed her around the small circle, ending the impromptu dance with a kiss. "Hello Mrs. Rodriquez. Are you happy?"

"More than I thought possible," Crystal whispered in his ear.

·♥·♥·♥·♥·♥·

*JOIN MY NEWSLETTER LIST to receive the latest news and updates! Or visit my website (www.bonniephelpsauthor.co m) to join.*

*Thank you for reading MY ARMY RANGER. I hope you enjoyed Crystal and Cam's story as much as I enjoyed writing it. If you did, I would greatly appreciate you leaving a review on Amazon here or the review site of your choice. Reviews are crucial for any author and a line or two about your experience can make a huge difference.*

·♥·♥·♥·♥·♥·

I THOUGHT THE TEXAS Kincaids series was finished with Cam and Crystal's story but her brother Wayne refused to be silenced. He'd spent all his life living in the shadow of his accomplished sister and cousins – now it's his turn to shine. In MY QUIET HERO meet two people each trying to find their own path but end up finding each other in the process. Want to know more? Read the book description below.

·♥·♥·♥·♥·♥·

**SHE'S READY TO START** living her life. He wants to be his own man. When fate brings them together, will they find a home on the range?

Kitty Langford craves independence. After spending her youth raising her siblings, the fierce older sister longs for the freedom she gave up. But when she leaves Oklahoma for Texas to at last taste independence, the spunky gal finds herself stranded on the side of the road... until a handsome local with kind eyes and capable hands changes everything.

Wayne Kincaid yearns to be seen as an equal to his accomplished cousins. Though he mortgaged his ranch to pay for school, the soft-spoken vet has a solid side-business raising animals to supply fur for the artisan yarn industry. He's determined to both get out of debt and prove himself. He never expected that Kitty holds the key to making his mark.

As Kitty falls hard for the dependable animal doc, her mischievous siblings discover her whereabouts and play a prank that backfires badly. And after two of his prize goats go missing, Wayne fears his new love could be hiding a relationship-ending secret.

Can the couple comb through their tangled troubles to find happily ever after under the Lone Star sky?

*My Quiet Hero* is the heart-warming fifth book in The Texas Kincaids contemporary romance series. If you like self-assured women, strong and silent men, and steamy chemistry, then you'll adore Bonnie Phelps's beautifully woven tale.

Buy *MY QUIET HERO* to give passion a voice today! READ an excerpt below.

# Excerpt from "My Quiet Hero"

♥

AS THE FEED PELLETS rattled into the trough, the goats scampered over for their evening meal. The musky smell of hay and animals hung heavy in the air. Kitty had a soft spot for the sweet and cuddly sheep. The alpacas brought a smile to her face as they hummed among themselves and approached people with big, curious eyes. But the goats had stolen her heart. Their spirit of fun and exploration struck a chord with her.

It was like watching the person she wanted to be. She was working on that. It was a slow process. Coming to grips with being abandoned by her parents had left a slew of trust issues in their wake. She also knew she had to stop feeling responsible for her siblings but so far hadn't been able to let go of the weekly calls to see how they were doing. She hoped that time and distance would eventually reduce the worry she carried like lead weight in her heart. With a sigh, she pushed her hair back and returned the scoop back to the feed storage bin.

The two sets of working dogs sat just outside the barn door watching the activity. The majestic Great Pyrenees pair, Chief and Sadie, were tasked with protecting the goats. Joy and Lively, the Border Collies, kept the sheep from straying and made sure they were in the barn and accounted for each evening.

A hay bale landed on the far end of the goat barn with a solid *thunk*. Wayne bent to clip the twine holding the bale together. Kitty paused to admire the way his jeans hugged his long legs and firm backside. The muscles bunching and releasing in his arms and across his broad back were an endless source of fascination as he broke the bale into the square, thin flakes that would supplement the pellets.

He straightened and caught her staring. Those oh, so kissable lips tipped up in a cheeky grin. "Enjoying the view?" Tossing a flake in her direction, it landed at her feet in a puff of dust. "No dinner till the job is done. Get a move on it slacker and fill up that hay feeder."

"So that's how it's going to be. You steal a few kisses and you think I'll turn into your willing slave?" She pulled on the hem of her t-shirt so it pulled tight against her chest.

Wayne swallowed and a lazy smile crept languidly across his face. "A man can dream."

Kitty approached him slowly. Like she'd seen in the classic black and white films she'd watched long ago with her mom. Those stars had known how to hold a man's attention. The heat flickering in his eyes emboldened her. Maybe she did too. Stopping in front of him, she leisurely walked her fingers up his chest. Anticipation zinged through her body like a bolt of lightening. She'd been on a slow boil since that kiss before they left San Antonio. Her body heated and antsy. "And what are you going to do if I don't?"

Wayne sucked in a breath and his eyes darkened further. Capturing her hands, his work gloves rough against her skin, he said, "This." Lowering his lips to hers, the kiss repeated what his eyes were telling her. Heat. Passion. Wanting. For her.

She opened her mouth and their tongues moved as though the rumba was playing in the background. Slow and sensual. The intimate Latin beat of the dance poured through her body to an internal melody. The hands caressing her back moved in time to the song in her heart. He must be hearing it too.

He'd kissed her before. Every time they were together. Kissing was part of the equation. A pleasure. A thrill. The newness of a man putting his lips on hers frequently did not seem to be wearing off. On the contrary, she'd become quite a fan of the activity.

Something was different this time. Like he'd shifted gears from first to fourth and had pushed the gas pedal to the floor. And boy, did she want to take this ride with him. Wherever the road led. Her gears had shifted as well. When his arms pulled her tightly against his body, she felt the bulge in his jeans press firmly into her belly. Electricity shot up her arms. Heat pooled at the juncture to her thighs. He peeled off his gloves without breaking contact.

Kitty gave herself over to the sensations bombarding her. Fingers slid into her hair. The gentle tug of his hands fisting. Knuckles pressing against her scalp. The angling of her head so his lips could explore the sensitive skin along her neck and under her ear. Her breasts tingled. Her bones turned to liquid fire. Sensations all new—but not new. Somewhere embedded in the far recesses of her mind a light flickered then burst into flames. Old and primal emotions burrowed deep into the core of her being embraced the awakening.

Her back bumped up against the rough barn wall. Wayne groaned and his hands drifted down her arms. Fingers intertwined with hers and his forehead touched hers. His breath whispered hot against her face.

"I can't get enough of those sweet lips of yours, but I'll be honest with you. I want more. I want to make love to you." Releasing her hands, he cupped her face. His thumbs glided over her cheekbones with a feather-light touch.

She closed her eyes and inhaled his scent. Barn, and hay, and masculine sweat. Certainty swept through her. She tensed. Did she have any idea what she was doing? Intimacy led to...trust? Was she ready to trust him completely? If she didn't tell him everything after they made love—and she was sure that was where they were headed—would that end their relationship?

"If you're not ready, there's no pressure. I can be a patient man. You're worth waiting for." He arched one brow and trailed a finger down the side of her face. She shivered as sparks raced up her spine. "However, if you do feel so inclined..."

Lacing her fingers behind his head, Kitty guided him until their lips were a hair's breadth apart. "I'm ready. Here. Now." Her heart pounded. She'd never been this bold and never felt so right. Tell him. Not tell him. She'd figure out the answers to her questions later.

"You sure?"

Kitty closed the gap and let their lips touch. "I'm certain."

Buy *MY QUIET HERO* today and give passion a voice!

# Also by

STAND ALONE BOOKS
Julia's Star

SERIES
### The Texas Kincaids
My Rodeo Man: The Texas Kincaids Book 1
My Sexy Veterinarian: The Texas Kincaids Book 2
My Texas Heart: The Texas Kincaids Book 3
My Army Ranger: The Texas Kincaids Book 4
My Quiet Hero: The Texas Kincaids Book 5
### Building on Love
Welcome Home: Building on Love Book 1
Serenity's Garden: Building on Love Book 2
Sold on Love: Building on Love Book 3
### Matchmaking Ghosts
More Than Pretty: Matchmaking Ghosts Book 1
Hold Me Tightly: Matchmaking Ghosts Book 2

# About Author

Rumor has it that Bonnie began telling stories at a very early age. Photos exist of the author toddling around the corner of the house covered in mud babbling about magic rabbits leading her through the garden. Her parents were amused – until they discovered she had also walked across the newly poured cement patio – which only added fuel to the fire of her passion for writing. From then on, her active imagination continued to churn out plots and character sketches always wondering how different people would behave in similar situations.

Bonnie used her writing skills throughout her professional life as a fundraising and communication executive for several nonprofits. She enjoyed the chance to tell and share the story of worthy organizations. In the late 1980s, Bonnie authored a syndicated column in several California newspapers in which she shared the experiences and misadventures of life as a wife and mother. The jury is out on whether or not her children always appreciated her candor. Because Bonnie has romance in her soul, she also worked as a Wedding Planner for several years. Absolutely loved it!! She craves anything sweet, revels in any chance to travel, and is addicted to tracing her family's roots. A native Californian, the author lives in Northern California with her husband.


SIGN UP FOR MY NEWSLETTER Once a month you'll receive the latest news about my books. I also love to share what's happening in my life, what I'm reading, and what's cooking in my kitchen – along with a favorite recipe.

Learn more about Bonnie and her books at her website: Bonnie Phelps Author

Have a question or comment?
Send Bonnie an email: bonnie@bonniephelpsauthor.com

Connect with Bonnie:
Follow me on Facebook

# Acknowledgments

Thank you to my critique partners – Elsa and Dawn – for reading multiple first drafts and helping fine tune my manuscript. I take each and every suggestion to heart. Thank you also to my fellow Romance Writers of America friends and colleagues, especially my Yosemite Romance Writer and Sacramento Valley Rose Chapter mates. Your friendship and well-aimed head slaps makes each book I write better. A special thank you to my content editor, Anna J. Stewart. You rock! Your guidance takes my writing to new heights. Finally, thank you to my proofreader, Dayna Hart for polishing my manuscript and making it print ready.

Printed in Great Britain
by Amazon

56836744R00078